DISHA

THE ULTIMATE DIRECTION

Dr. Ddharaniikota Ssuyodhan PhD (Hon.)

Copyright © Dr Dharanikota Suyodhan 2025
All Rights Reserved.

ISBN
Paperback 979-8-89744-995-8
Hardcase 979-8-89961-600-6

This book has been published with all efforts taken to make the material error-free after the consent of the author. However, the author and the publisher do not assume and hereby disclaim any liability to any party for any loss, damage, or disruption caused by errors or omissions, whether such errors or omissions result from negligence, accident, or any other cause.

While every effort has been made to avoid any mistake or omission, this publication is being sold on the condition and understanding that neither the author nor the publishers or printers would be liable in any manner to any person by reason of any mistake or omission in this publication or for any action taken or omitted to be taken or advice rendered or accepted on the basis of this work. For any defect in printing or binding the publishers will be liable only to replace the defective copy by another copy of this work then available.

A tribute to all the women who have suffered for being women.

Acknowledgement

*I'd like to dedicate this book to my parents, **Shri D Dhananjaya** and **Smt Usha Rani** who are blessing me from the world above, who have taught me everything I know in this life, and who have inspired me to achieve great heights.*

*I have heartfelt gratitude to my son **Dhanush SriHaas** for inspiring and motivating me to take this up and write the book that I had always dreamed of.*

*The sincerest thanks to my dear wife, **Dr. Hima Deepthi**, for being patient with me and allowing me to pursue my passion.*

I bow down to my Gurus and send love to my family and friends who stood by me and supported me.

<u>Lastly, to all those social workers, lawyers, doctors, police, and security forces who work day and night to provide justice to women.</u>

Contents

Foreword 1

Justice is a fundamental pillar of any society! It is the guiding principle that ensures the rights of individuals are protected and that crimes do not go unpunished. But what happens when justice is delayed? Worse still, what happens when justice is denied, manipulated, or obstructed by those in power? Disha is not just a book—it is a powerful and necessary conversation about the flaws in our legal systems, the resilience of those who fight for justice, and the moral dilemmas faced by those sworn to uphold the law.

Dr. Ddharaniikota Ssuyodhan, a renowned legal expert and global advocate for gender justice, is uniquely positioned to write this book. With over two decades of experience working with NGOs, women's rights organisations, law enforcement agencies, and national and international institutions of repute, he has not only analysed these issues but has actively engaged in shaping policies and driving awareness. As a panellist on TV debates and a contributor to discussions in media and legal forums, he has brought to light the complexities of gender-based violence and legal shortcomings.

When I first met Dr. Ddharaniikota Ssuyodhan, we had an engaging conversation on these pressing issues. What struck me most was his innovative thinking, practical approach, and ability to move beyond the usual rhetoric. He brought fresh perspectives, grounded in real-world experiences rather than theoretical arguments. Over time, as I followed his debates and discussions on numerous occasions, my initial impression was further augmented and reinforced. This led to frequent discussions between us, where we would analyse regional, national, and global developments related to these challenges, and I understand that Dr. Dharani has a penchant for interacting with people who are not only passionate about this subject but also who have a diversity of opinion. His deep understanding of the subject and ability to connect different dimensions, legal, social, and institutional, make him the perfect voice for a story like Disha.

At the heart of this novel is Inspector Rithika, a fierce and uncompromising officer whose belief in the judicial system is tested by a case that shakes her to the core. She is forced to confront an unsettling question: Is the law always enough to deliver justice? Alongside her trusted colleague, Inspector Muthuswamy, and supported by her family, she embarks on a journey that is not just about solving a crime but about understanding the very foundation of justice itself.

Having worked in international legal and human rights institutions, I have witnessed firsthand how gender-based violence and systemic injustice transcend borders. Across continents, women continue to face legal loopholes, delayed trials, and silencing by those in power. This book echoes the voices of countless survivors who demand action, not just in courtrooms, but in policymaking, enforcement, and social transformation. The solutions that Disha calls for, such as specialised women's police stations, gender-sensitive legal procedures, and speedy justice mechanisms, are not just fictional aspirations but urgent national if not global, necessities.

I deeply appreciate how Dr. Ddharaniikota Ssuyodhan masterfully blends real-world facts, urgent social issues, and legal complexities with gripping twists and compelling narration. The way he weaves together truth, suspense, and thought-provoking dilemmas makes Disha both an engaging novel and a call to action. Dr. Ddharaniikota Ssuyodhan has skillfully combined legal expertise, social activism, and powerful storytelling to craft a novel that forces us to confront our own beliefs about justice, morality, and accountability.

– Srinivas Kumar Left Indian Civil Services (1993 batch) and joined the United Nations, working with the UN for the last 24 years in senior positions in seven countries; presently Chief of Stabilisation and Livelihoods Unit of UNDP, Philippines.

Foreword 2

With crimes against women on the rise, DISHA is a novel that should make us sit up and think. The novel is fast-paced, and the reader would want to move from one chapter to the next, waiting to get to the bottom of a series of bewildering and unnatural murders. Is it one person, or are there a group of people behind these gruesome killings? Dr. Ddharaniikota Ssuyodhan doesn't give us time to think. He pushes our curiosity with yet another murder. It is easy to read, and with the numerous crimes in our neighbourhood, the novel reads like what's happening next door.

Dr. Ddharaniikota Ssuyodhan advocates independence for women and being the legal professional that he is, he puts the complexity of a system of law that is ineffectual under the limelight through DISHA. This is a warning as much as it is a quick-paced series of who-dunnits that keeps the reader on edge. The thin sliver of romance that lines the entire narration is not highlighted until towards the very end of the novel, and when Rithika finally buries her head in Muthu's shoulder, the reader is also a little relieved that all through the tension, all through the action, the determined, single-minded police officer is at last shown to be human too.

Dr. Ddharaniikota's novel reads like a film: a string of killings, and the police are clueless—or are they? The realities of life are depicted through a series of everyday incidents but highlighted to make us think a little more than usual. Is life as innocent as it seems? The horrible truth that Rithika finally manages to get out of herself is a relief not just to her but to us, the readers, as well. The age of innocence is a thing of the past.

Dr. Ddharaniikota Ssuyodhan has written in a racy and fast-paced manner, but at the core, questions are raised—questions that push us to think. The core question is, "Can you take the law into your own hands?" DISHA is an answer. But it is an answer that should frighten every person who does not do his or her duty conscientiously.

DISHA is a comfortable read with some uncomfortable questions. I wonder when Dr. Ddharaniikota plans to write his next novel. It will just as surely make us think.

– Dr John Varghese, Principal, St. Stephen's College, and Professor of English

Chapter 1

Fingers Morphing Pleasure

The walkie-talkie blared in the police jeep, "Ma'am, we are ready with the body."

"Arre! I told you we are reaching the hospital! Don't you understand it is raining cats and dogs in the dead of the night!" Inspector Rithika snapped at the speaker, her head churning due to the lack of visibility.

That night, the police jeep was rushing through the thunder on Pantheon Road in Chennai when Rithika asked the officer to stop. She got out of the car and took the wheel in her hand. During an emergency with a difficult journey ahead, Rithika believed in only her own rash driving skills on bumpy roads.

A murder was reported for the second time that month and both had similar types of killing. Rithika and her police team had inspected the murder place for two hours, where they found a computer processing a morphed video, and a daughter crying beside the dead body that she called her father. Other than this, the police team that was given the charge of this case was perplexed at the tidiness of the crime spot. Not a single drop of blood, saliva, or hair was to be found even after a thorough search.

"The murderer cleaned the area before leaving, ma'am," said Bablu, the constable, for the third time as he held the handle above his head to balance himself through rash driving.

"Oh, really Bablu! Do I look blind to you? Or deaf?" Inspector Rithika screamed at him. "I saw the clean murder spot and I heard you say that twice before!" She turned the wheel around at once, and the tyres screeched through the puddles, splashing water on the car parked nearby.

"It is just that, I am shocked," Bablu said again, calmly sitting in the passenger seat as if he trusted Inspector Rithika with his life.

"I will shove your police stick in the right place, and you will never get a shock, ever!" she said and stopped the car, the windshield wiper looking as aggressive as her.

The walkie-talkie beeped again, "The team is still searching at the murder spot. We hope to find something."

Rithika asked the constable to open the murder file and look for more clues as she pressed on the brakes with force in front of the hospital, the jeep sliding across the road and stopping with a jerk. The police officers sitting behind held onto each other for life when Bablu screamed, "Puppy!" and Rithika pressed on the brake, skidding through the mud and bringing the jeep to a halt.

Rithika Murthy crashed into the windshield. The vehicle was halted, and there was silence. All they could hear was the windshield wiper moving in the quietness of the night that was broken by Bablu's call, "Mam!"

"Ma'am!" said another officer from behind.

All the officers called her out, worrying that something had happened to her. With a moan, Rithika stood up straight, tucked a strand of her hair behind her ears, and tried to look around.

Seeing her face full of anger, Bablu started explaining, "Ma'am, there was a… a puppy on the road and I saw it suddenly… so I just… and I screamed… I am so sorry…" he shivered.

Her breath, which was rapid in rage, calmed down as she understood his pure intentions, and her brows straightened. Keeping the file on the dashboard, they got out of the jeep, and her shiny black boots landed in the mud. The constable held an umbrella over her head, and she started walking towards the Government Hospital Egmore.

The structure was old, with aluminium sheets and rods lying outside. The rusty iron door clanked as Rithika banged it open to enter. She had to cover her nose due to the filthy smell emitted from every corner of the hospital, which hadn't been cleaned for weeks. The muddy footprints of everyone coming from outside added to the dingy look.

"I think the murderer should come here to clean the hospital as well," joked the constable with his palm covering his nose.

Thunder bolted in the sky as she reached the morgue room and saw the impatient looks of the medical staff. All she could hear was water leaking in the distance, as silence encapsulated the room. On a table in the middle of the morgue lay a fat body that looked 50 years of age, pale and dark with straight black hair freshly dyed and a large mole on the nose. A yellow light lamp hung over it that needed some cleaning for brighter illumination.

Rithika spread her palm towards the constable who handed her a tissue, and the senior medical staff said, "Please don't touch the body…"

At Rithika's one glance, he went silent, and she started wiping her boots with the tissue. As she cleaned her foot, she saw the hand of the body and realised that all the fingers were chopped off. She stood straight and looked at the other hand, only to find it without fingers, too. She started wiping her other feet and asked, "What did this man do?"

"He was in digital technology – clickbait, YouTube videos, things related to that…" the police officer present at the morgue before Rithika entered answered her. In his early thirties, Muthuswamy had a dark wheatish complexion but a sharp nose and was always ahead of his time. "Do you need more tissues before we start inspecting the body?" he asked her rhetorically, and Rithika gave him a side-eye look.

Her head tilted as she handed the tissue to the constable and took a deep breath. "The Cleanliness of the surroundings gives a clear mind to work," she said to no one in particular and looked around at the messy room.

"Miss Police Inspector, Crimes Division, Rithika Murthy," said Muthuswamy. "Our government hospitals are always full of bodies from this area, the only hospital that is available 24/7 and…"

Rithika's gut boiled at this taunt, "I know how much the government is working for us and for themselves... I don't need your..."

"And they started…" the constable whispered in Bablu's ears with Muthuswamy. Rithika shot a look at him, and he went numb.

Sitting in his daily chair in the comfort of his home, Raghu was hastily typing the codes on his keyboard to morph yet another video for money. Recently, he used the pictures of a beautiful girl called Rita from his daughter's college, created an erotic video, and posted it on YouTube. After this incident, Rita committed suicide as it had slandered her image in the city like wildfire. Although Raghu's own daughter was very sad about this incident, he couldn't stop doing this work for the greed of Gandhi notes that he received every week.

His daughter entered the room with a sombre look, placed a cup of coffee on his table, and said, "I am going to meet my friend Mona. She is still not over Rita's death… suicide…" she stammered.

Raghu nodded without even looking at his daughter, a blank Excel sheet open in front of him, feigning to type numbers on it. And right when she walked out of the house, banging the door behind, unaware of the deeds of her own father, Raghu reopened the software he was working on.

Under the photo frame of his daughter's convocation day with all her best friends hanging on the wall above him, he saw Mona's same photos from that frame, added up together on his computer to form the face of the woman giving herself pleasure in the video.

The medical staff cleared his throat and said, "This is the second time we are receiving such a case with all the fingers chopped off. Why would anyone cut off the fingers? And how? I mean…"

"Obviously after the murder," Muthuswamy said matter-of-factly, "he would have killed him and then sat there like a psycho, chopping off each finger, taking in the fun of doing it, feeding his brains with madness of the moment as he slashed each finger one by one…"

It had been raining for a week, and thunder shot again in the sky. As the video was being processed on the YouTube channel for upload, Raghu took a sip of coffee from the cup and smirked at his daughter's photo frame above, "I am doing this for us, my baby," he talked to her photo, "You said you want to go to Australia for further studies, we need money for that, don't we?" he chuckled.

CLANK!

A vessel fell in the kitchen with a loud bang, and Raghu's brows narrowed. He looked at the screen, still processing the video, and got up to check. Entering the kitchen, he rolled his eyes at the vessel fallen on the ground, bent down to pick it up, and with the clink of it being placed on the platform, he heard a shrill voice, "Rita wanted to become an IPS officer and Mona, she was studying to become an engineer before she was eaten up by the shock of Rita's suicide."

Raghu turned around to see a tall figure covered with a black balaclava, the eyes were bloodshot. The person was wearing a black hoodie and black gloves, holding a sharp, shiny knife. The person looked like a walking coal, with a voice as shrill as a ghost.

Raghu's breath turned shallow as he asked, "Who are you? And how did you enter my house?" He stuttered with fear.

The person, looking like a live coal, held Raghu's shivering fingers and said, "You do too much work with these fingers, they must be tired, aren't they?"

"No," he pulled back his hand. "Who are you? What do you want... I will give you..."

"What will you give me? Money?" the person chuckled. "And you think I need that? The money you earned by using these women's bodies without their consent?"

The person in black held his fingers again, moving slowly near him, caressing his fingers with his knife. Raghu said, "Let me go, please. Are you sent by the goon head Taala? I told him I would pay my loans. Please don't harm me..."

"No, I will not harm you," the person leaned in closer and whispered, "I will just give rest to your fingers..." looking into Raghu's eyes, the murderer went silent for a moment. Raghu's face turned sweaty, his breath turning flimsy when the murderer pulled his fingers with great force, thrashed them on the platform, and slashed the knife on the fingers.

"Aargh!" Raghu screamed.

"But there are no signs of killing," the medical staff told Rithika, "No other part of his body is harmed, only his fingers chopped off."

"How can someone die by just chopping off the fingers?" Muthuswamy asked.

"And how can someone be so intelligent?" Rithika rolled her eyes and asked the medical staff, "Excessive bleeding, unbearable pain, and…" She looked at her constable, "As you said, the room was clean of any mess, so I am sure that the murderer let him die in excruciating pain, bleeding uncontrollably while cleaning the room."

"Seems like a real retard, that murderer…" said the constable, nodding his head.

After inspecting the body and asking routine questions of the medical staff, the head doctor said, "You will receive the post-mortem report by the day after tomorrow."

Rithika and her team left the morgue at 7 am and decided to sit in a cafeteria for coffee and idli while discussing the issue. The constable opened the file kept in front of him and went through the case when he saw a headline in the newspaper kept on the table.

Fingers Chopped Off and Went Viral on the Internet!

"There has been a similar case in other parts of India recently!" he said, picking up the newspaper.

Muthuswamy opened a news website on his phone by searching for a similar headline and read aloud, "A Mohali man's fingers were chopped off in broad daylight. Punjab Police has registered a case against 3 people who were seen in a video cutting off the fingers of a man allegedly over the suspicion that he was linked to the murder of their friend."

"But why chop off the fingers?" asked another constable.

"Why did this dead man murder the murderer's friend?" asked Rithika.

Muthuswamy shrugged, "Not one, but many more similar cases have been found," and he read further, "In another article, it reads, 'The Uttar Pradesh Police on Friday found the headless body of a woman with four of her fingers missing in Banda district. The woman, aged about 35-40 years, was partially clothed and her head was found at some distance from her body, according to the Superintendent of Police Ankur Agarwal.' He sighed, "God save us!"

Rithika blinked her eyes and shook her head. "The evil side of humans is just so..." she whispered, nodding her head, which was bowed down in distress.

Their constables got up to smoke while she sat there rubbing her forehead and blinking her eyes rapidly. She took a sip of coffee and said, "We will go to the depths of this case and find out the murderer!"

"Yes, we will, don't worry," Muthuswamy said softly.

Rithika looked up at him while he stared at her gently. Slowly, Rithika shifted in her seat and said, "Aren't you hungry?"

Muthuswamy cleared his throat and said, "No, I am not, but are you fine?" He tapped her shoulder and then withdrew at once, unsure if he should have done it.

"Yes, I am good, let's order something…" she got up, "I'll just have a smoke and come…" she said and walked away. Muthuswamy nodded at her and as she left, he closed his eyes in embarrassment.

Chapter 2

Declining Carnal Years

With a small round face and the wrinkles of a 68-year-old man, and a neatly shaved face with white dentures making him look a little younger, Sahil Dada was young at heart. Early in the morning, he would dress smartly in his little bungalow located at higher altitudes of Darjeeling and go for a walk, meet his friends, and then visit other social gatherings in his town. Even at this age, he was famous among women, even the young ones.

That morning, as he was going home from the coffee shop, he bumped into a lady wearing a light-yellow chiffon saree that hugged the curves of her body, "I am so sorry, uncle!" she said in her sweet voice.

Sahil looked at her with a smile and said, "It's okay!" and then noticed her waist looked voluptuous. Her black blouse peeked from behind the saree, and Sahil couldn't help but try to make conversation, "You look in a hurry, are you searching for someone?" he asked with a smile, showing off his white dentures that hid his age.

"Um, yeah, my friend is coming," she said and looked around. "Oh, there she is!" She pointed at a lady, smiled at Sahil, and walked away. Sahil turned around to look at her from behind as her long hair brushed against her back.

That night, Sahil couldn't sleep. He looked at the photo of his wife hanging on the wall and said, "She was as alluring as you are," putting his hand under his blanket, he kept thinking about the lady in the yellow saree.

The next day, Sahil kept making rounds of the coffee shop after his morning walk. He shopped at the market for groceries, met his friends, and played a game of cards. He kept hoping to run into that goddess again, meet her again, and talk to her more.

Days went by, but he couldn't find her. He asked the coffee shop owner if he had seen the lady in the yellow saree with whom he had collided a few days ago.

"It seems like you are too excited to bump her—I mean into her," the shop owner giggled.

"I am just a gentleman who cares for the women of his society," Sahil smirked. She seems new in the area, and it is my duty to take care of the new pretty ladies in our town. " He winked at the shop owner and tossed an almond from his counter into his mouth when he heard some women giggle.

Sahil turned around and saw the lady, this time in a black saree that made her wheat skin look brighter. She had tied her hair up in a bun, revealing her thick, long neck and smooth shoulders.

Without wasting another second on his imagination, Sahil approached her, "Hi!" he said enthusiastically, taking a glance at the other woman with her and then fixing his eyes on the lady in black, "I forgot to ask your name that day," he said.

The lady smiled, "Sorry? Do I know you? Uncle?" Her brows narrowed, and the shop owner chuckled from his desk.

Sahil shot killer glances at the owner and said, "Don't you remember? We bumped into each other that day?" he said, "You seem like you are new in this area, aren't you?"

"Oh yes, I remember you. How are you?" she asked.

Sahil put out his hand and said, "I am good, and you?"

"I am good too," she shrugged.

"People call me Sahil, and you?"

"Shruthi," she smiled.

"Do you come here regularly?" he asked.

"Quite frequently," she said.

"Oh, this is boring. If you are new here, you should see the gardens of our town and the green hills," he said excitedly. Whom do you plan to go with?"

Shruthi shrugged and looked at her friend, "My friend, but..."

"But you don't know how to go, right?" Sahil said. "Don't worry, I would love to be of help to such beautiful ladies."

Sahil told the women about the beautiful places in the town, and both of them looked excited to explore the wonders of nature. That afternoon, as it wasn't sunny, they decided to go to the nearby garden and take a look at the enticing flowers grown there. Shruthi was not only thankful but also charmed by Sahil's warmth as he narrated the history of the place to them.

The next day, he took them to the hills that grew the rare lavenders, and it looked no less than heaven. Shruthi loved the hills and said that she wanted to come here again.

After a few days, her friend was busy with family commitments, so she asked Sahil if they could visit the mountain hills with lavenders again. Sahil happily agreed and visited the medical shop to get ready for his first solo outing with Shruthi.

As they walked along the fields, talking about their life, Sahil told her that his wife died two years ago, and she said that she divorced her abusive husband last year.

"Oh, you must be so lonely," he whispered softly. "Don't you feel that you need love?" He brushed his fingers on her arm, and as she nodded her head slowly, he leaned in, his face getting closer to hers but then crossed over to hug her.

Sahil hugged her warmly as a friend, confusing her with his gesture, and whispered, "I am always here, don't worry, Shruthi!"

Shruthi tightened her arms around his body and said, "I know!"

As they walked further, Shruthi pointed in the farther direction and said, "Let's go to the end of this field!"

Sahil looked in that direction and saw that there were tall grasses with wide trees at the end, just perfect for his dream time with the voluptuous lady. He readily agreed and walked with her, talking about how he had helped some orphaned kids last month and then paid the coffee shop owner's loans to get out of his debt.

"You are such a kind-hearted man," Shruthi said, and Sahil smirked, thinking how these fake stories always enticed the women.

As they reached the end of the field, there was nothing but walls of long grass and lavender. Shruthi had worn a lavender-coloured saree that day, and Sahil kept staring at her, "You know you look like lavender today, camouflaging in this field," he moved in closer to her as she tucked a strand of her hair behind her ear.

Sahil could see her blushing and moved his fingers on the skin of her hands. His face leaned closer to her mouth, and he held her chin with one hand. His other hand wrapped around her waist as he pulled her closer. Her hands rested on his chest as she tried to block his move any further, but the 68-year-old man was strong enough to hold her wrists tightly and move them behind her back.

"What do you want?" she whispered in his ears. Sahil dug his face into her neck and bit her shoulder. Shruthi trembled, closed her eyes, and he bit her again. He bent down and pulled her legs, making her fall on her hips. With a smile, Shruthi saw him climb onto her body, ready to be devoured by the animal in front of her.

With the sun setting in the background, the dark night encapsulated the hills. The lavenders looked dark grey under the moonlight like a demon swinging in the cool breeze of the night.

The next day, Shruthi visited the coffee shop with her friend. She had a plate of *Upma* and coffee and chatted for about an hour, telling her how beautiful the hills were.

"So?" her friend asked softly, "Did you guys finally do it?"

"Do what?" Shruthi asked with narrowed brows.

"Do not try to fool me, I know how desperate you have been since your divorce, and you were clearly charmed by the old man!"

On hearing this, Shruthi slapped the palm of her friend and shushed her, "Keep quiet, it's a secret!" They giggled.

A few days later, when she visited the shop again, the owner approached her with a distressed look.

Shruthi looked at him and asked, "What happened?"

"Uhm, ma'am, actually I wanted to ask, uh-mm, have you seen Sahil?" he asked.

"Sahil?" she turned red. "No, I have not seen him since last we met that day. I mean, we went to the hills. They are beautiful, you know, that's why," she chuckled awkwardly, her cheeks turning red. "We came back in the late evening and since then, it has been a few days. I haven't seen him."

The shop owner looked worried. He kept glancing at other tables aimlessly, and Shruthi asked him, "Is everything alright?"

"Yaa," he wiped his forehead, "Actually," he paused, his breathing getting rapid, "No, he hasn't come to the shop for so many days now."

"He must be resting, he is an old man now!" Shruthi's friend joked and scoffed under her breath.

Shruthi stroked her friend's arm softly and said, "Not that old, I tell you honestly!" The ladies sniggered, covering their mouths with their palms.

The shop owner realised what Shruthi meant and walked back to his desk. He knew very well how frisky Sahil was and decided not to ask these ladies about the situation.

A few days later, when Shruthi was back at the shop with her friend, she saw the owner sitting quietly at his desk, still looking worried. She approached him and said, "Your friend hasn't come yet? I came yesterday, but you were also not there, and neither is Sahil seen anywhere these days. Is everything alright?"

The shop owner said frantically, "Sahil has not come home for more than a week now," he nearly whispered. Shruthi's jaws fell open as he continued, "His family has filed an FIR, and the police are searching for him everywhere, but he is nowhere to be found," he said and looked around quickly. "And I am scared that if the police ask me anything, I will get so scared with their introspection that they will doubt me, even though I am innocent!" he peeped out of the café and said, "My heart races whenever I see the police officers strolling outside my shop here."

Shruthi's fingers covered her mouth, and she felt a hand on her shoulder. "Ah!" she nearly screamed, jumping around to see who it was.

Seeing her friend, she closed her eyes and took a deep sigh of relief.

"What happened?" the lady asked.

Shruthi pulled her hand and took her out of the café without replying to her friend. They hired a cab to go back home.

"What is happening?" her friend asked for the hundredth time, and finally Shruthi replied, "Since the day I met Sahil on the hills, and…" She paused before continuing, "Things happened between us, you know… he disappeared after that, his family has filed an FIR, and the police are searching for him!"

Her friend's eyes widened, "You mean that you are scared of the chances of being caught by the police as the prime suspect just because you were the one he last saw?"

"Exactly!" Shruthi said, and her breath turned rapid. Her nose started sweating, and she sat down on the bed. Her friend wrapped her hand around her shoulder. Fear crept up their bodies as they couldn't think of any plan to save themselves. They just had to wait for fortune to smile at them.

For the next few days, they avoided leaving the house and working only from home. On their way to buy groceries, they did not go anywhere near the café or meet the shop owner.

A month of torture later, Shruthi visited the shop owner, thinking that the situation must have cooled down, and she wanted an update on the case.

She saw the owner working on his computer and approached him smiling, "Hi!"

Without looking up at her, he said, "Yes, tell me. Has it been long since you came here?"

"Yes," she said, fidgeting with the paperweight on the desk, "Um, I wanted to ask if there is any..."

"He is dead," the owner said flatly. "The police found his body behind the lavender hills." His eyes turned misty.

Shruthi's expression turned stoic. She couldn't understand how to react as the owner continued, "His body was pale and wounded at every possible place, his eyes were out of their sockets, and his mouth had turned violet," he whispered to her, "The police were shocked at the condition in which he was found. His mobile phone was set on fire, and his family is traumatised!" Hearing this, Shruthi felt like vomiting and rushed into the washroom.

After a few minutes, she came out and settled at a table. The owner served her a cup of coffee and said, "I believe you; you are innocent. " He looked at her, "Because he was no gentleman himself," he stared at her intently.

Shruthi's brow narrowed in confusion as he continued, "Two years ago," he murmured, pulled a chair beside her, and said softly, "Two years ago, Sahil was convicted of raping a 13-year-old girl."

Shruthi looked at him in utter shock, her eyes wide like those of Goddess Mother Kaali as he continued, "Not once, but he raped her, molested her for a month!"

Shruthi's hands covered her mouth, and her eyes turned misty. The shop owner nodded slowly and said, "Sources have it that he gave her twenty rupees every time after he was done with his evil deed and asked her to keep her mouth shut. Otherwise, he would kill her!"

Shruthi's eyes started watering, and she started sniffing into her palms.

"I am sorry," he continued, "You must be feeling dirty that you spent a night with such a man for fun, but..."

Shruthi did not listen to him completely and rushed out of the table, storming out of the café and walking up to her house. Her mind was rattling, and she couldn't think of anything when she heard her friend call her, "Shruthi!"

She came and stopped beside her. She was shocked to see her cry, "What happened?"

Shruthi hugged her tightly and kept crying bitterly, howling in pain and holding her friend tightly.

Chapter 3

Water Dripping On Desires

Tony, a slim young boy in his early twenties, got off the bus and looked at the lush green mountain and trees climbing up the hills. He stretched, moaning in excitement, and said, "Welcome to my new life!"

Kuki, a short boy, tapped his head and said, "What new life? You are the same old shit!"

Raseed and Chakir laughed as Tony explained, "Why not, bro? We have received the opportunity to work on a YouTube video with an advance payment of twenty thousand each!"

"I agree!" Raseed said as he started walking towards the auto stand.

As the four friends walked towards the hotel where their new employers had asked them to accommodate them for the YouTube video shoot, Kuki wrapped his hand around Tony's waist and said, "Brother, are you sure that it is safe for us to be back in Mandi?"

Raseed and Chakir looked at him and then exchanged glances with each other.

"What are you even talking about?" Raseed asked, walking up to Kuki.

Kuki's mouth turned dry, and he gulped down the fear, "You know what I mean. Our last vacation to Himachal last year was so much fun, but..."

"But are you scared of being caught for the mischief we did a year ago?" Raseed questioned with furrowed brows.

"Was it just mischief?" Kuki asked.

Raseed, the tallest of all, stopped in his spot and glared at Kuki aggressively. He pointed a finger at him with so much intensity that his arm started shaking as he said, "One more word about that day…" He tightened his teeth, "And you will hear it from me!" He turned around and walked away, punching the air, followed by Chakir and Tony.

Kuki's forehead started sweating as he followed them into the hotel. The boys checked in and entered their room. It was a mid-sized room with two beds and two mattresses. The walls were chipped in every corner, and there was leakage from two corners of the room under which buckets were kept to collect the water dripping. In another corner of the room was a table with a broken leg and a bottle of water that seemed so old, as if no one had checked in the room for ages.

"What is this even?" Raseed frowned at the condition of the room. "We are going to shoot for a video, and this is what we get for travelling so far. Is it all on our expenses?"

"Exactly! This is outrageous!" Chakir said. "We should complain to the channel!"

"On it!" Raseed dialled the number on his cell phone, and the person picked it up after three rings. "Hello… yes, we have checked in the hotel room as per the location you sent us on WhatsApp. I really have to describe how bad the room's condition is. It is just not habitable..." Raseed stopped momentarily and heard what the person on the other side said. "Oh... really? Okay! Uhuuh..yeah, that sounds, that sounds totally interesting... hmmm... hmm, I understand your idea, yes, yes, it is very creative and ... ahaa, correct, I am on it, I'll explain to my boys, yes, thank you! No problem!"

The other three men looked at each other in confusion. Raseed, who had called the channel angrily to complain about the room, was now smiling and agreeing with them. He kept his phone on the bed and settled on one of the mattresses, "We will have to stay here, boys."

"Huh? Why, but? Don't you see how bad..." Chakir's brow furrowed to its extreme when Raseed interrupted him.

"They said that they gave us this room in such a bad condition on purpose. It is for the preparation of the role that we will play for the video," dusting the mattress that he had just sat on, Raseed sneezed twice and got up to change. "They say that such a dire condition will help us to emotionally prepare for the torturesome role that we are going to play. As we all know, it is an experimental video about crime and torture, and hence, we are going to get paid so well for it..."

"God knows what torture they will put us through!" Kuki said as he tried to catch the water dripping from the ceiling on a finger.

"Don't worry, guys!" Tony said cheerfully. "It will be exciting! I am sure! Because where there is money, there is only fun!" He raised his hands in the air.

"I agree with you, my friend!" Chakir gave Tony a high-five. "Don't you see, guys?" he looked at Raseed and Kuki. "We were small-time labourers, and then we sold our ancestral lands in the village to start our own shop and earned good money from it. Then, we were able to make that trip last year to Mandi. That trip gave us the idea to start making reels, where we now have five thousand followers in a year! That is why we got to work on a YouTube video! This channel has only 500 followers, but they paid us advance money because they assured us that their idea is amazing and it will bring all of us at least one lakh followers!"

"Yes, who doesn't like to see torturous videos?" Tony said. "People love such reality videos."

"Hmmm... God is with us!" Kuki said. "For the hard work that we have done!"

"Exactly!" Chakir said. "Stop being so negative and rise," he pulled Raseed's hand. "I am hungry now, let's have a nice lunch before our shoot in the evening."

They took a bus to a restaurant and ordered all their favourite dishes, followed by desserts. After a hearty lunch, they started searching for the address where they were called for the shoot.

"From here, we need to take a right," Raseed said.

"Sir, there is no studio here..." said the autorickshaw person.

"It must be an open shooting space," Chakir said. "Not a studio then."

"Yes, possibly," Raseed said as the autorickshaw reached a lonely lane with a broken concrete road. The four friends exited the vehicle, and the sun was scorching hot, melting them from head to toe.

"Let's go quickly, the sunlight will make me sweat and spoil my face," Kuki said, covering his eyes with his palm.

"What's more to be spoiled there?" Chakir raised a brow, and they all laughed.

Kuki rolled his eyes and started walking in the direction they could see a road, "There is only jungle on these two sides," he looked around, "What will be here to shoot if not a studio?"

"Just keep walking, brother," Chakir pushed him softly from behind. Stop asking so many questions and look at the map; we are already there."

As the four walked a few more steps ahead, they spotted a broken house at the edge of the hill. The lawn was crawling with dried and dead plants, and they could spot some rats running haywire.

"I hope there aren't any snakes here," Kuki held Tony's arm.

As they walked further, they reached near the house, which gave out an eerie vibe. The creepers from the lawn had started wrapping over the bungalow; it had broken walls that looked burnt down. The silence of the place was eating their ears when suddenly Chakir broke the quietness and asked, "Are you sure this is the correct place?"

"I am not going inside!" Kuki took a few steps back.

"Me too!" Tony joined Kuki while the other two stopped moving ahead. After a lot of anticipation, they knew something wasn't right, and their body language changed as they went in the opposite direction of the house when their phone rang. The sound of the ringtone was a Bhojpuri song, but it echoed through the empty silence like a horror music. Kuki jumped into his place out of fear.

Raseed checked his mobile phone and said, "It is the YouTube channel calling me..."

"Tell them to book a studio!" Kuki screamed. "What is this place? I am not going inside!"

Raseed picked up the call and said, "Hello... ahaa... yes, I understand, right... okay... hmm... but can't you at least? Okay, got it... um... cool, we will come..."

"What? I am NOT going!" Kuki shouted, and Raseed showed him his palm to quieten him. He kept his phone in his pocket and said, "They are inside this house and have seen us from there. They explained that this is the perfect eerie place for creepy experimental videos. They have assured us not to be scared and that it will be fun to shoot here. They feel this will surely boost the views. They have even kept photos of various Gods in case the energy inside is negative or bad energy is lurking around."

"Huh?" Kuki shrieked.

"Don't worry! They have taken all the precautions for us and the team," Raseed wrapped his arm around Kuki's shoulder and gently pulled him towards the house. "It is time to become rich, guys!"

"Do they have all the shooting equipment ready?" Tony asked.

"Of course, they must be having it; otherwise, how would they shoot, and what would they be doing inside?"

"They sound quite professional," Tony said.

"But what if..." Kuki stammered.

"Stop with your negativity!" Raseed scolded him.

"He is only our negative energy, throw him out of the video!" Chakir sounded annoyed.

"But I am... guys..." Before Kuki could say anything else, his three friends walked towards the house through the long dried grass tickling their legs. It gave out the sound of the dead plants being crushed under one's feet as they moved nearer to the house. The wooden planks of the wall were broken from their place and were hanging down from one side. Some of them were burnt like coal, and they had a foul smell coming out of them. Raseed opened the door slowly, and a rat ran out through the sill. Chakir held Tony by his arm while Kuki held Raeed as they took a step inside the house.

It was pitch dark inside even though the sun outside was burning bright. Right on entering the house, they were in the living room space with broken seats and springs. A small black cat with yellow eyes had made it to her home and four tiny kittens were feeding her milk. She meowed at the four men and kept staring at them. The side of the house that looked burnt from the outside was covered with a huge bedsheet cloth like a wall. The other side looked like a kitchen with a platform and some china vessels, broken and scattered on the floor. There was a window in the kitchen area that gave out some light for them to see something. Behind the kitchen, they could see a spiral staircase that went up to the first floor with a wooden railing. But it was dark, and they could only imagine what there would be up on the floor.

"Hello? Is someone there?" Raseed called out, and at once, they started hearing footsteps approaching them. Kuki and Chakir clenched their friend's arms tighter and leaned in closer.

"Hi! This is Chang! How are you guys?" a girl in her thirties emerged from behind the cloth wall. She wore tight skinny jeans, and her high heels made a clanking sound as she walked.

She smiled at all the men, revealing the pink shade of lipstick, and shook hands with them. "It is so nice to meet you guys finally!"

The boys were happy to see such a beautiful girl. All their fear vanished at once as they stepped to greet her and shake hands with her. Kuki came in the end to shake hands, but by that time, she had started speaking, and he missed the chance. He felt left out and ignored by her as Chang said, "I am the head of the channel, and I will guide you all about the shoot."

While she asked about their journey and Raseed tried to act cool, saying they had fun travelling to this place, Kuki kept staring at her loose white shirt tucked in neatly and a strand of her hair kissing her cheeks when she finally looked at him. A big smile painted on his face, but then she looked away and continued talking, "I am glad that you guys like Mandi. So, this is where we are going to shoot," with her arms spread in the air, she took a walk in the living room towards the kitchen and turned towards them, "Isn't this the best place for a horror and thrilling shoot?" she said loudly. Her voice echoed through the passages of the house.

As the men nodded in agreement with her, Kuki raised his hand and said, "But, Miss Chang, don't you think this house has a really creepy vibe, as if something had happened here?"

Chang's smile faded, and lowering her gaze, she looked around. "Yes, there is because... this house... it has a past..."

"What past?" Tony asked at once, his forehead wrinkled.

Chang sighed deeply and said, "For today, you guys have had enough of a spine-chilling experience. " She giggled softly, gave a one-sided smile, and said, "Let's save some for tomorrow!" She jumped excitedly and ambled towards the big cloth. "I'll be back!" Leaning out of the cloth wall, she said, "Do not come on this side!" and disappeared.

The four men looked at each other and smirked. They knew what they were thinking. How beautiful the girl is! Her perfect curves and white skin shone like a moon. Her long, soft hair and big, juicy lips painted into a perfect beam, showcasing her linear teeth.

Chang came out with some ropes and said, "Come, follow me, it is time to shoot our first video!"

The men followed her into the kitchen when Raseed asked, "Wait a minute, where is your team?"

As Chang inserted the ropes in each of the iron loops on the wall, she explained, "Oh, they are behind the curtain, sitting silently, watching us from the hidden camera. You see, if they come here and meet you all, you guys will not feel alone and stranded. This will reduce your fear, and it will not come out in the video. And I don't want you guys to feel less scared; I want you guys to be afraid for real. Afraid of being here in this haunted house and for that, you shouldn't feel the presence of any human that may make you feel safe." She tapped on Raseed's shoulder lightly and asked, "Is that fine?"

Raseed turned red and nodded his head.

"But you told us that there are people here, what difference will that make? We know we are not alone," Tony said.

"And you believed me so easily?" Chang stared into his eyes, and his smile faded away. There was a stoic expression on their faces, and Tony clenched his fingers into a fist. He looked at his friends when suddenly Chang chuckled in a high-pitched tone that sounded scary enough to go against her personality.

The boys took a deep sigh of relief, "Come on, guys, just don't pay attention to the thought that people are sitting behind the curtain. They are given strict orders by the channel producers that they cannot make a single noise."

The four men looked at each other while Chang observed the doubts marked on their faces and said, "Come on now, sit here all of you," she said, and they followed her instructions, their bodies moving slowly and less interestingly when she added, "Once our experiment is done today, we will credit you the next amount tomorrow."

Hearing about the money, they all turned energetic and let her tie them willingly.

"I will tie your wrists together with this rope above your head and also your legs so that you cannot move during the experiment," she said as she tied them one by one, "and the first experiment is the 'Chinese drip torture'!" She fastened the ropes tightly and stood in front of them.

The men looked at each other in confusion and she explained further, "A drop of water will fall on your forehead every 5 to 10 seconds. The hidden camera in front of you will keep recording your reactions. There are a total of 6 cameras hidden to capture you from every angle. This is the Chinese drip torture!" she clapped her hands. "All the best!" She jumped in her place with a little shriek of excitement.

The men looked at each other's faces with their hands tied up and burst out into a peal of laughter. Chang looked at them in confusion as the men kept laughing loudly.

"What is this even? Chinese what?" Tony asked in between his chuckles.

"This Chinese torture sounds as lame as the Chinese products we use!" Kuki commented, snorting in between his laughs.

Chang smirked from the corner of her lips, "Time will tell how bad this experiment is!" She held her waist as a drop of water fell on their foreheads, and Chang walked away from there.

"Where are you going?" Kuki called out to her.

"To leave you alone with your funny torture!" she called back, and her voice faded away.

The men giggled under their breath so as not to offend Chang anymore. As the water kept dripping on their foreheads, they kept discussing what they were planning to do with the money they would earn in the future. One wanted some foreign girls as sex slaves, another wanted to buy a car, another wanted to buy a house, and one wanted to pay off his parents' debt. The water that was dripping from above was not falling at an equal length of time. Sometimes, it would take 5 seconds, sometimes 10, while at other times, it would take 20 seconds. An hour had passed, but they could not anticipate the next drip. The anxiety of the sudden cold sensation that they felt while they were talking annoyed them so much that they deviated from the subject and couldn't pay attention to what the others were saying.

In the next two hours, they stopped conversing and just paid attention to the drips, thinking that it would get over soon. Their foreheads turned cold, while their bodies turned hot due to exhaustion and stress. Their mental state was affected by anger, but they thought that it was a petty thing to get frustrated about, so they tried to control themselves and stay calm.

"How long will this go on for?" Chakir asked after one more hour.

"How does that even matter? Are you exhausted already?" Raseed chortled.

"It is annoying. I am frustrated now. I want warmth," Kuki said.

"Grow up, Kuki; how does a drop of water annoy you?" Tony said. "Here, my hands are paining from being hung and tied up, and you are worried about the water?"

"Yes, I am worried about the water, so what?" Kuki said loudly. "Don't you dare call me immature just for sharing my feelings!"

"Hey, guys, chill," Chakir said.

"No!" Kuki sounded annoyed. "I am tired of hearing all the time about how childish I am and..."

"What are you tired of, huh?" Tony interrupted him, "Yes, you are childish, and we are tired of hearing you cry all the time! ALL THE TIME!"

"Then go away! What is the need to roam with me?" Kuki shouted.

"I didn't even want to go with you, it was Raseed who asked for you."

"Shut up, you guys! Will it sound good if the girl heard us brawling like this?" Raseed interrupted. "What impression will it leave on her?"

"You worry about yourself, not us!" Kuki screamed at Raseed, "At least I know how to behave with girls!"

"Oh, shut up, Kuki!" Raseed said. "Stop this. You are no saint yourself, okay? So do not…"

"I am not a saint?" Kuki shouted. "At least I do not force a girl down!" he spat at Raseed.

"Kuki!" Chakir screamed.

"How dare you!" Raseed said.

"Guys! Stop it!" Chakir shouted.

"You don't teach us!" Raseed screamed at Chakir. "You brought that girl!"

"And he started again!" Kuki smirked. "And whose idea was it to play with her?"

"If you had so much of a problem, you shouldn't have touched her!" Tony shouted.

"Shut up! All of you! What are you saying? We are being recorded!" Raseed yelled at the top of his lungs.

Kuki's breathing was rapid when Chakir whispered, "Did the team members hear us?"

"I don't think so," Raseed said. "I hope not…"

There was silence for the next few minutes as they waited for someone to come running to them due to their quarrelling. They tried hard to pick up the sound of footsteps approaching, but rats broke a pin-drop silence at intervals, running haywire through the stuff lying around and the sound of water dripping on their heads at uneven frequencies.

Another hour passed in silence. The four men did not discuss anything further. They were tired of waiting for someone to hear their brawl. But then they sat silently, anticipating the next water drip on their heads.

Another hour had passed. They were tired of waiting. Their hands were frozen from the cold and pain. Their minds had stopped working. They were slipping into unconsciousness.

Raseed gathered the courage to call out to someone, "Chang! Are you there? How many more hours will we have to sit here like this?"

"Who watches such long YouTube videos anyway?" Tony asked.

"They will fast-forward our video and then upload it, you idiot!" Kuki spluttered angrily.

"Shut up, you fatso!" Tony spat back.

"How dare you?" Kuki screamed and tried to get up, but his tied legs did not move. He realised that his legs had turned hard due to soreness, and he couldn't feel his legs. "My legs!" he screamed. "Chang! Please come and help me!"

While Tony laughed at Kuki, teasing him as a fatso, Raseed and Chakir also tried to move, but the knots of the ropes were tied really well.

"I cannot move!" Chakir whimpered. "It's enough! Where is Chang?" he demanded. "Chang! Where are you? Come back!"

"Yes!" Kuki shouted. "I don't want your money, just come and untie me! Chang!"

"Chang!" Tony bellowed loudly from the depths of his lungs, but their voices only echoed through the empty, dirty house. It had turned dark outside. The sun had set, and they couldn't see each other's faces.

"What is happening?" Kuki asked. "Why is Chang not coming?"

There was silence. No one had an answer. The quiet house was now encapsulating them as their breaths turned rapid.

"Are we kidnapped? Was this a sham?" Kuki was on the verge of crying.

"CHANG!" Raseed howled like a wounded wolf. But there was no reply. "Enough!" Raseed tried to move in his place and searched for something sharp. "Is there anything near you guys? Anything sharp like a knife or any weapon?" He tried to get up, but his legs had cramps. He kept rolling his limbs from right to left and back to get rid of the cramps. "Come on, guys, find something, anything! A piece of metal, glass, or stone…"

They all rolled their eyes and tried to search with their feet, but they couldn't find anything. The place where they sat was clean and tidy. Not even a speck of dust. Due to the darkness, they couldn't see anything around them; they couldn't see if anything useful was kept nearby when they heard footsteps approaching.

"Chang?" Kiku called out, hoping. Oh, thank God you came back! This Chinese torture is just too much now. Please untie us now. I am hungry, too!"

The footsteps were the same as Chang's, like heels clattering on the wooden floorboards. They could smell a girl nearby with the same strawberry perfume scent they had sniffed previously, and as the footsteps stopped, they knew she was standing right in front of them.

"Chang, untie us, now the camera also cannot record us," Raseed said impatiently.

"I am sure you guys understood how difficult this experiment was," Chang said finally, her voice sounding firm without the pinch of bubbliness in it as she had earlier.

"Yes, yes, totally, it wasn't funny like we laughed previously at its name and nature," Chakir said.

"Yes, it was very difficult, I am sure you will get millions of views on this," Tony said. "Now, please untie us!"

Her heels walked CLICK CLACK on one side and then on the other side. The men waited impatiently, giving her the time to untie them when she said, "Do you know why we started with this experiment?" They heard the screeching of a small wooden table being pulled by her, and she sat down on it in front of them.

"For views!" Raseed said. "How a torture that seems so small and easy is actually so torturous for REAL."

Chang laughed, "Yes, for sure, and what else can be the reason?"

"I don't know," Kuki said. "Please untie us, I am hungry!"

"Yes, I will untie you, Kuki. Please be patient. This is the last ordeal of the video. We have a night vision camera, so please, you are being paid for this," she said slowly and firmly.

A silence spread among the fretful men, and the energy turned patient in that room. Chang took a deep sigh and said, "I would like to tell you guys and our viewers here about this house," she got up and took a walk, "As I previously showed you the house in the video, recording every corner of it, you all saw that a particular part of this house is burnt. The woods are turned into coal, and there is a foul smell coming from it," she kept walking, "Do you want to know how and when it got burnt?"

"Yes," Tony said at once, and all the men turned their eyes towards him, their guts crumpling with anger.

"A beautiful family of three lived in this mansion," Chang started immediately. "The father had inherited his father's business, and they were one of the rich families of the state. The mother, a simple housewife, and their daughter, their heart and soul. But one day, their daughter hadn't returned from a party that she was attending. The parents waited for her all night, but she didn't come. Then the next day, in the morning, they saw a video of their daughter playing games with men." She paused, and Raseed's throat dried as she continued, "They didn't understand what kind of games they were playing but tried to locate the place by looking at the background of the video carefully. Soon, they reached the spot in their car, and guess what they found out?" Chang whispered the last words, "Her body was lying naked, bleeding between her legs, and a rod inserted there."

Rasheed and Tony started panicking and moving in their places, trying to rid themselves of the ropes as Chang continued, "And this wasn't it, the shed under which she was lying had a broken roof, and the heavy rains all night had led to the water dripping on her face all night."

Kuki and Chakir's eyes widened as they also started understanding where Chang was going with the story and tried to free themselves from the ropes, their limbs frantically moving and pulling the locks. At the same time, she narrated further, "The doctors gave the obvious news and said that she had died an hour before they had arrived," there was silence before she spoke in an eerie whisper, "The viral video of her made everyone in the town say that she was at fault. Playing weird games with FOUR strangers, that too men is going to land her in such a condition." Her breath was raging, "She was only 17 and innocent. Yet she was questioned for not understanding the worldliness at such a young age!" she sat down on the table in front of them, "Her father picked her up and got inside the car. He didn't allow the police to complete the investigation and the next news that this town received was this house burning on fire."

"Leave us! You fraud!" Raseed screamed.

"We didn't do anything!" Kiku pleaded.

"Of course, Kiku, you didn't do anything," Chang said sarcastically. "You just had fun for two minutes because all your friends were doing the same. Used a woman's body like a sex toy, ignoring her feelings, her consent, and her cry for help!"

"But who are you? What do you want from us?" Chakir asked.

"Justice!" Chang said loudly.

"Then hand us over to the police, why are we here?" Tony asked.

Chang started chuckling, and slowly, her chuckles turned into a peal of laughter. "You know, when I visited this burnt house, I noticed that this pipe hanging above you, which had been dripping water for hours on you, was broken. While that side of the house was burnt to ashes, this pipe was broken due to heat pressure. And I realised that this gas pipe still has some elements of its supply mixed in the water."

The men started smelling themselves and realised that they smelled of natural gas used in kitchens. They started screaming, "What do you want to do?"

"Please leave us!"

"Forgive us, please!"

"I have to take care of my parents, please!"

They pulled their hands and legs to release themselves from the knots, but nothing worked. They pleaded with

Chang to forgive them and assured her that they would get arrested but that they would be allowed to live now.

"We will surrender, but leave us now. Call the police, but don't do anything!"

Chang lit up a matchstick with a flick that finally showed her beautiful face. She had tears in her eyes but a strong determination to take revenge. "May your crotches burn in hell!" she said and threw the matchstick towards them.

"Aaarghhhh!" they screamed at the top of their lungs. With a satisfied smile, Chang moved behind, seeing them burn and agonise in pain, scream for life, and cry one last time.

Chapter 4

Connecting The Dots

Inspector Rithika Murthy was on her first vacation in five years of service to the people. Sitting on the balcony of her hotel room, which overlooked the beautiful Darjeeling, she sipped green tea with her parents.

"Finally!" her mother sighed. "We got our daughter back after years!"

Her father sniggered as Rithika rolled her eyes, "Mom! I live with you guys! Why do you keep taunting me as if I live seven seas away!"

"Living with us physically is not sufficient! You have to give time to your parents!" her mother snapped.

"I do! But you just want to taunt me in the time that I give you!"

"I am not..." her mother uttered, but her father showed his palm.

He became the referee, "Stop it, you two! Let me hear the birds chirping!"

As Rithika nodded her head, she picked up the newspaper to read.

"See now, she wants to check the news in the country again," her mother said. "She is never with us, always working!"

"She is always serving," her father corrected her mother and a big smile painted on Rithika's face.

"By the way," her father asked, "What happened to that case of a man murdered with chopped fingers?"

"Nothing, Dad," Rithika said as she took a bite of a cookie, "We caught a murderer, and he was in judicial custody. But the evidence couldn't prove him guilty, and the police closed the case due to a lack of evidence or witnesses."

"He was a criminal himself, right?" her father asked. "And what about that man's daughter? She must have been shattered!"

"Hmm..." Rithika continued reading her newspaper when her eyebrows narrowed, and she brought the paper closer to her face. Reading the news more intently, her lips mouthed the words quickly, and her eyes moved rapidly across the paper.

Her parents observed her change in energy. She had clearly become the police officer from the daughter that she was a few seconds back as her father asked, "What is the news?"

Rapist Of A 10-Year-Old Girl Found Murdered Like An Insect: Cops.

She read the headline, and her parents turned serious to listen further.

A 68-year-old man has been found in the most horrific condition on the hills of Darjeeling. His face was nearly unrecognisable, and his hands were crooked as if they were bent by a beast. His private parts were set on fire, and his mouth had remnants of firecrackers. The town is shocked by this news, but there are also mixed feelings among the people.

According to the police and medical department, this man was arrested two years ago for allegedly raping a 10-year-old girl for nearly a month in the Darjeeling district.

'According to the FIR, the incidents took place when the girl would go home from her school. The accused, a local resident, used to give her ₹20 every time after raping her and threatened to kill her if she revealed the rapes to anyone,' a police officer said.

The incident came to light after the girl's mother found her crying uncontrollably, and the child finally narrated the events to her mother, who then lodged an FIR.

There was silence for a moment as the family let the horrifying news sink in. They couldn't sip their teas anymore, and the sandwiches lay there turning stale. It seemed like the birds had also stopped chirping upon hearing about the events and hid themselves in the trees.

Rithika slowly turned the page and continued reading.

"There is a mixed reaction among the people at large over the two connected incidents that took place. On one hand, people are glad that someone took it upon themselves to fight such an evil monster after he was bailed out due to his connections and wealth. But on the other hand, many do not agree with this inhumane treatment of even a monster that is against the laws

of the country. What is your opinion? You can send us a text on number 888088."

Rithika's mother nodded her head, "I agree with the murderer. He did the right thing. He took the laws into his hands for such culprits who have the power to buy the cops, the system, and the government officials!"

Looking at the vast green field in front of her, Rithika took a deep breath and said, "I do not agree with you, maa. I am sorry, but a system is put in place for a reason, and crime and corruption also need to be fought only under the gauge of that system."

TRING!

Rithika's phone rang, and she saw the name Muthuswamy on it. Rolling her eyes, she picked up the phone and said irritably, "Hello?"

"Whoa! Someone doesn't like being disturbed during her vacation," Muthuswamy chuckled.

"And what is the reason behind disturbing me?"

"Hmm..." he cleared his throat and turned serious. "One of my batch mates from Mohali, Punjab contacted me regarding the case of the finger-chopped man."

"Uh-huh?" she encouraged him to speak further.

"So, I had a word with him when we were working on that case in Chennai because you were concerned about the similarities it bore with cases of fingers being chopped in Punjab and Uttar Pradesh. And as you know, your concerns are my concerns," he chuckled, and Rithika rolled her eyes as he cleared his throat and continued, "So, I asked him to research the history of all the victims who were murdered by chopping off their fingers, and it turned out that some had rape charges against them while some had molestation charges!"

Rithika's eyes turned wide. "Muthu!" she exclaimed. "I just read a news in the local newspaper of Darjeeling that…"

"You are reading the newspaper on your vacation?" he interrupted.

She paid no heed to his comment and continued, "I read that a 68-year-old man was brutally tortured and killed, and he had rape charges against him two years ago…"

"So, you mean…"

"Yes, those finger-chopped cases can be connected to the murder of a 68-year-old man because even he was a rapist," she said and went deep into her thoughts.

"So, what do you plan to do now?" he asked, but there was no response. "Hello? Rithika madam?"

"I'll call you back," she said, getting up from her chair and rushing out onto the balcony and into her room.

Her father followed her and asked, "Are you going somewhere?"

Rithika did not answer. Her mind was racing with thoughts, and her father understood that she wasn't mentally present to hear his question. Quietly, he walked out of the room, and Inspector Rithika Murthy was back to duty as she collected her revolver, tucked it behind in her denims, and wore a long coat over it, walking out of the hotel with her handbag to find out about the truth.

✱ ✱ ✱

The next evening, the police station in Chennai was bustling with criminal chaos as a thief gang had recently been apprehended by the team, and a frenzy of media houses had gathered outside the station to interview the sub-police inspector, the mastermind behind catching the gang. The gang was in the lockup, and they were going to have their trial the next day. Inspector Rithika left her cabin after completing her research work that day and walked into the police station with the file in her arms, checking on the mayhem going on, when one of the thieves commented, "Hey, hey! I wish I was caught by this lady police! I wouldn't have wanted to be let go of her then!" and his gang men laughed heartily at his comment.

Rithika ignored his sleaziness and went straight to meet the Inspector General (IG) and knocked on his door.

"Come in!" he called out from inside, and she opened the door to walk in. "Ah! My most able inspector! Rithika, how are you?"

"I am well, sir, and you?" she took a seat in front of him.

"I am absolutely amazing! Well, but you will have to take care, huh? Your sub-inspector did a great job; he could be promoted soon to your level," he chuckled.

"I will be glad, sir. It would be fun to work with him on the same level."

"Well, in that case, I am relieved to hear that!" he smiled widely. "By the way, weren't you on leave? For... for a vacation in Darjeeling? Am I right?"

"Yes, sir, you are right, but um... actually..."

"Yaa, tell me," IG said, sitting up straight. Seeing her serious, he intertwined his fingers to listen to her keenly.

"Sir, I am sure you remember the murder case of the 50-year-old man whose fingers were chopped," she started, looking straight into his eyes.

"Yes, yes, I do. It was an open-and-shut case since we couldn't find solid evidence against the murderer."

"Yes, sir, but um, if you look at the other similar cases all over the country, there were murders with fingers being chopped and as per our research, all those victims had rape or molestation charges against them," IG's eyebrows furrowed as she continued, "So I really think there is a connection between these murders or maybe between the murderers."

The IG leaned back in his chair, and his fingers tapped on each other as he thought for some time before opening his mouth to speak, "I agree with you, Inspector Rithika. You may be right about the connection between the murders, but, um... as you know the law perfectly well, I would still want to remind you that this is our... your suspect. There could be a connection, but where is the proof? We need solid..."

"I know, sir, my suspicion may not be solid evidence, but there is such a steadfast link to all of them. All three murders have taken place by chopping off the fingers of the victims, and the victims have the same past. What are the odds of them not being related to each other?"

"Does this reveal who the murderer is?"

"No, but we need to start with a joint CBI inquiry for these cases, from all three states where the killings took place," she looked hopeful.

"Rithika, you know it is not easy to get the CBI involved in any case; we need to have a strong basis."

"But sir,"

"Look, I understand your concerns and the way you have used your mind is very smart, but it is not enough," he sighed. "I wish I could do something to..."

"Let me take on all these cases and work on it,"

"But on what basis do I reopen the case?"

"That is a *connection*!" Rithika said loudly. Her breathing was rapid, but then she realised right away that it was wrong to raise her voice like that.

Looking as if he did not expect this behaviour from her, he said, "You are dismissed," and switched on his laptop, not giving Rithika another look. His finger moved on the touchpad.

Slowly, she got up and walked towards the door, opened it, and turned around to look at her senior again, expecting some understanding. However, he refused to pay attention to her. Disappointed in herself, she walked out and closed the door behind her.

"Aha! Look, she is back! The Katrina Kaif of police officers!" commented the thief again, "Come on, lady, lock me up with you!" A roar of laughter echoed through the prison when a constable banged his stick on their cell and screamed, "Shut up! Don't make noise! It is not a place for entertainment!"

"But I can make her scream for entertainment!" he remarked again, and his gang giggled under their breath.

Rithika shot a glare at him, unable to ignore his comments anymore. Her face quivered with rage, given that her mood was already in a bad state as she walked up to the locker, pulling up her sleeves.

"What did you say?" she asked him through clenched teeth, standing upright and pulling up another sleeve.

Looking at the vex etched on her face, the thief thought for a second before replying when his gangmate remarked, "That he can make you scream with pleasure!" He started snorting, holding his belly, his eyes watered from all the laughing.

"Raghu!" Rithika called out to a constable, "Open the door!"

With shivering fingers, the constable followed her orders when the criminal said, "Is she ready for it? For real?"

"Shh!" another gang member hushed him as they swallowed the ball of fear in their dry throats.

Right when the door opened, Rithika stormed inside the locker and grabbed the member by the neck, who was making sleazy remarks: "What did you say, huh?"

"Nothing, I was just…" he stuttered to give an excuse when her hold on his throat tightened, "Repeat!" she said very firmly.

He shook his head. "No, I am sorry, I will not…"

"I said, REPEAT!" she screamed at the top of her lungs and punched the criminal right in his face, making him fall to the ground. "First of all," she said in between breaths, "You are shamelessly locked up in the cell for a crime and on top of that," she picked him up by his collar and slapped him hard on his cheek. "You have the audacity to pass such immoral comments! You piece of shit!"

"Madam!" two female constables entered the cell and held her, "Please let him go, he is not worth your energy."

"No! I am going to kill him! How dare he?" She was about to pounce on him when the constables held her and pulled her out of the cell, "Please ignore them; had they such manners or common sense, they wouldn't be inside; please control yourself."

Breathing heavily, Rithika did not let them get the best of her as she walked out of the building and went straight up to her cabin.

"Hey!" she heard someone call out to her, but without looking at who it was, she kept on stomping further with heavy legs. "Hey, Rithika!" he called out again.

Rithika turned around to find that Muthuswamy had just arrived at the police station. He then followed her and stopped in front of her. "Where are you going so angrily?" he asked.

"I don't know!" she roared, her voice harsh. "I don't understand why they are not ready to reopen this case?"

"Shh! Chill," he showed his palm to calm her down. "I'll explain to you, come with me," he pulled her by her arm softly and walked up to his car. "Sit, we'll need to go to a private space to discuss this."

Without thinking much, she settled inside the car, and he drove off. "Look," he said calmly, "I know it is so important to you to solve this case, and all the similar ones linked to it, but you will have to understand the practical aspect of it as well."

"What practical aspect? What is above the lives of the people who were wronged? And what is above the law against which that murderer is killing all those criminals?"

"The politics?" he asked her rhetorically, "The leaders who control every step that we take, who control the emotions of the people and tell us that their win is above everything else." He said with a stoic expression, and it all came crashing down upon her like the biggest reality check.

Rithika was stunned for a few seconds, trying to process this information. Even though she knew that she couldn't do anything, given that her system was controlled by them, her heart did not accept it. A fire burned deep within her chest, urging her to take action against all wrongs.

"So, what do you expect me to do? Just sit quietly and see the crime taking place?"

"No, we will do something, I promise. You know I am with you," he looked at her with admiration, but she kept staring ahead, deep in her thoughts.

He sighed, "See, I will try to contact…"

"Where are we going?" she interrupted.

"Nowhere, just on a ride to talk."

"I need to go home,"

"Okay, I will drop you…"

There was silence as he turned the car left and took the highway to her place.

"By the way, you just came to the police station, where were you?" she asked suddenly, breaking the silence.

"Yeah, um, yeah, actually, I was late," he forced a smile. I was working late at night, so…"

Rithika didn't pay much heed to what he said, and right after the car pulled over to her house, she got out and said, "Thanks for dropping me off. I'll contact you soon."

"Any time," he smiled.

Walking into her house, she saw her dad cooking lunch. Without a word to him, she went inside her room and sat on her bed, her elbows resting on her lap, her fingers crossed, her face resting on them.

Rithika's mind was racing from one case to another. The connection between them, and the cities that they took place in. The possible reasons behind the murders and the link of the murderers. What could it be? She couldn't understand other than one thing.

A social work against the sexual abusers!

But is this the right way?

She thought deeply when her conversation with her mother in Darjeeling repeated in her head.

'I agree with the murderer, he did the right thing. Took the law into his hands for such culprits who have the power to buy the cops, the system, and the government officials!'

Her mother had said.

'I do not agree with you, maa. I am sorry, but a system is put in place for a reason, and crime and corruption also need to be fought only with the help of that system.'

She had replied to her mother with utmost pride and confidence in the system. But Muthuswamy's words were now shaking her faith in the system. The reality check he gave was making her mother's words true to her. Yes, there are people buying into the system. Yes, there are people getting bailed out with the power of money and connections to the leaders.

YET, is taking the law into our hands the right thing to do?

She questioned herself again and grabbed a pillow, covered her mouth, and screamed into it in frustration. Breathing heavily, she turned on the bed and lay down when she felt a palm caress her hair, "What is confusing my strong lady?" her father asked.

"I don't understand, papa," she said in a defeated voice. "What is right and what's not? And what should I do to find out the truth?" Her breath shuddered.

"What is stopping you from finding out the truth?" he asked.

"The system. The leaders. The ones who should be protecting us do not want us to find the truth!" she clenched her fist. "And you know why? Only to protect THEIR image!"

Her father placed his palm on her shoulder and asked, "They do not want the truth to be out, but at least you can find the truth, can't you?"

"But what is the logic behind this? How will it help in just finding the truth and not putting it out?" she rubbed her face.

"Truth is the most powerful thing in this world. Once you find it, no one can stop it from getting public. No one can hide it anymore, no one can suppress it," he paused because she suddenly turned tranquil, listening to him more keenly. "Your job is to find the truth, and it is the universe's job to show the truth to the world!" he whispered firmly.

Rithika turned around and got up from her bed. Tucking her hair behind her ears, she asked, "Are you sure? Will it come out on its own?"

"It will, if you rightly fight for it, the universe will come together to help you. Just do not doubt it. Keep working for the welfare of the people, do not let the bad things demotivate you because good things are far stronger!" he shone a light within her that was being dimmed by the corruption.

She nodded with determination.

* * *

The next day, Rithika got up to get ready for the office when her mom came running into the room and said, "Check the news."

Rithika followed her and looked at her father sitting at the dining table for his breakfast when she saw the news channel showing their Chief Ministers happily talking about the police force's win in catching the murderer of the rapist. "I am pleased to inform the people of my state that we have caught the deadly criminal, the mentally unstable killer who chopped off the fingers of his victim!" he said into the eight mics placed in front of him.

The CM was then joined by the IG Balram beside him when the media person asked, "Sir, it took almost a month to catch this maniac killer, but do you think more people like him would be roaming around in the country? What is the proactiveness from the police department's side to stop any more of such killings?"

IG Balram replied, "The Chennai police force is working tirelessly 24/7, and we assure you that you all are safe. We have caught the lethal culprit and his gang after running behind them day and night."

The camera panned to the gang of killers that the police had arrested, and Rithika's eyes widened, "No!" she gasped, "They are not the killers!" she said, her brows furrowed.

"What do you mean, Rithu?" her father asked her.

As she stared at the faces of the men being taken out of the court in handcuffs, she said, "They are the gang of thieves! The police caught them this morning!"

Rithika pulled out her phone from her pocket, and before she could dial the number, he had called her at the same time, "Hello? Muthuswamy? What is going on? The gang they have caught is not…"

"I know, even I got the news just now. I didn't know that they were going to just blame them for what they didn't do…" but before he could complete his sentence, Rithika hung up the call and walked out of her house.

"Fight for the right, for the truth, my queen!" her father cheered as she closed the door behind her.

She was about to find her car when she realised that she had left it at the police station when she came home last night with Muthuswamy without thinking about anything, her mind clouded by the corruption going around. Stopping a taxi, she got into it and started calling the IG and the DGP.

No one picked up her call, and her impatience was rising. The early morning traffic tested her before she reached the station, which took an hour.

Paying the driver, she rushed into the station and went straight up to the IG's cabin. She knocked on the door restlessly and right after she heard, "Come in," she stormed inside.

The IG looked up at her in surprise and asked, "What happened early in the morning that you are looking so worked up?"

"They were thieves until yesterday, and now, suddenly, they are murderers?"

The IG removed his specs and kept them beside the laptop, took a deep sigh, and gestured to her to the chair in front of him, "Please have a seat."

Pulling the chair aggressively, she sat on it, her hands on the desk and her leg shaking impatiently.

"What is it that you want?" he asked, his brows raised.

"Why are the thieves caught as the murderers?" she asked slowly, emphasising every word.

"You know Rithika, elections are near and... that murder case was the headline of so many media channels, people were questioning the CM and the police force on social media, and," he sighed, "so... the minister wanted the killer to be caught as soon as possible."

"But they are not the killers!" Rithika said loudly, banging her palms on the desk, her breath turning rapid.

"Mind your voice," he said calmly.

"How can I?" she looked at him unbelievingly. "How can I stay composed when you catch someone just for the minister to save face? How can I stay quiet when you are not working towards finding the murderer?"

"Because that would take a few months... Finding the murderer and the elections are next month, they don't have time to wait..."

"I said I would find the murderer, but you did not allow me to..."

"Yes, because the minister had already said to publish the news of the murderer right away. They did not want to wait even for a week!"

"So, when I came to talk to you yesterday, you had already been sold to the minister?"

"Rithika!" he raised his voice. "Do not forget who you are talking to!"

"A corrupt police officer whom I looked up to until this morning, but now turned out to be someone else!" she screamed louder.

"You know very well the pressure on us during such times. I wasn't paid for this! I was threatened to be terminated!"

Rithika's breath slowed as she said softly this time, "But sir, this is an important case!" she said through clenched teeth. "It is not just the murders; it could be a racket for revenge for sexual...

"I don't understand why you are so involved in this case!"

"Because it is a matter of importance!" she screamed again, looking at her senior incredulously.

As her voice roared, there was silence in the cabin. He stared at her gravely as her breath moved her chest rapidly, her brows twitching in anger.

"You're suspended," he said, shutting his laptop, getting up from his seat, and walking towards the window, his back facing her.

Rithika had nothing else to say. She couldn't speak to his back, especially after he suspended her. What will she say? And how will she continue to work on this case during her suspension period? She was frozen yet shivering from anger. She couldn't understand what to do or how to explain to his senior that this case was so important.

She sat there waiting for some miracle to happen, hoping that he would turn around and talk to her, give her one last chance to speak out clearly and discuss. But he didn't, he did not budge from his position and Rithika had no choice but to get up and leave with heavy steps, banging the door behind her.

Chapter 5

Lust Over Breathlessness

A groggy-looking man in his early 50s walked out of his cell. His posture was slouching, and his white prisoner's dress with a couple of black stripes and a similar hat was larger than his size. He trotted through the passage while the rest of the prisoners ambled cheerfully. It was the monthly movie night where the prisoners enjoyed a Bollywood movie after dinner. The prisoners couldn't stop guessing which movie it would be tonight as they eagerly had their meal.

As they sat in the AV room with a big white cloth for the screen, the old groggy man sat in the back when someone called out to him, "Hey Ganja, what will you see from that far a distance? Huh?" Other prisoners called him Ganja, a word in Hindi because he was bald.

"Let him be Kaalin, he must have seen all the movies," said another guy, and his group started laughing.

As the room turned dark and the movie title appeared on the screen, Ganja felt hungry. He hadn't had his dinner properly because he hated the jail's food, consisting of two fat, unchewable chapatis and a watery soup of lentils with some vegetables that had more oil than the masalas. Such food troubled his stomach, and he got up from the middle of the movie and went to the washroom.

That night, Ganja couldn't sleep. Increased gut issues made him restless, and he needed his nebuliser. He got up and walked up to his prison cell door, calling the guard for help, "Listen, please, I need help…"

But the guard was asleep, and Ganja got scared. "Listen! Guard! I need my nebuliser!" he coughed. "I can't breathe!" He started banging on the cell bars. "HELP!"

The guard woke up with a start and asked, "What happened?"

"My… my nebuliser…" Ganja sat down, trying to breathe heavily.

The guard rushed to the medical box nearby for the prisoners in that row, brought out his pump machine, and gave it to him.

As Ganja breathed a sigh of relief, the guard asked him, "What happened suddenly that you needed it tonight? Weren't you fine for a few days now?"

"The food is killing me! It is garbage!" Ganja roared.

"Oh, so you want 5-star food here after committing a crime?"

Ganja looked at him sternly and said, "Even the law treats us humanely as prisoners, so we deserve good food!"

"Anyway, you need to fast, look how fat you have become! I don't know about breathlessness, but you will surely die of obesity!" the guard snorted, snatched the nebuliser from his hand, and walked away.

Ganja walked to his bed, feeling a little better, and lay down defeated. As he closed his eyes, he reminisced about the delicious food his wife had made and missed her.

The next morning, during breakfast, there was an announcement by the senior officer, "Hear, hear! Everyone! I was transferred to this jail a year ago, and since then, I have brought about some changes for the benefit of my prisoners. I allowed the monthly movie nights. I started with the first aid box in every cell section, and now, I am glad to see the discipline in this jail under my supervision."

The prisoners clapped unenthusiastically as one of the prisoners standing near Ganja said, "And he is happy with the money he takes from the food department that has reduced the quality of food we get." Ganja looked at him in disbelief.

"Arre... don't you know, he even earned from the first aid boxes by not keeping a sufficient supply of medicines in them," said another inmate.

"And today, I have come here to announce another programme that I have organised for the growth and development of you all!" waving his arms in the air, he pressed on the last two words, and there was a massive round of applause in the hall.

"Care Shakti NGO will come to this jail for a month from tomorrow. They will conduct various classes thrice a week for your development. Their teaching programmes include career counselling, motivation, positive thoughts, and spirituality. I hope you will all cooperate with them, learn new things, and become a better person."

As he completed his speech, the prisoners clapped until he left the dais and walked away with a wide smile and a broadened chest.

The next morning, the NGO arrived on time, sharp at 8 am, right after breakfast. The prisoners gathered in the hall when a lady in her early 30s walked onto the dais in a pink Kurti and white dupatta. A wave of whispers passed through the hall at the sight of the beauty of the lady with curly hair and a perfectly round face.

"Good morning, my dear inmates! I will not call you all prisoners or criminals because my job here is to make you feel more human and give you more confidence that you must have lost living in these four walls," she looked at the guards and the officer standing beside her. "Of course, I am not implying that your condition is pitiful because, in the end, it is your Karma that you all are here," she smiled and looked back at the inmates and continued, "But I just want to make sure that you are all comfortable with our team," she gestured at the women standing behind her. "My beautiful team of ten women who are here to teach you the truth of life," and there was a huge round of applause as she said, "And I am sure you must be happy seeing so many women after months or maybe even years!" she giggled, and everyone laughed with her.

"She seems fun!" said one of the inmates.

"Yes, I thought some old hags would come, but here is a wave of fairies!" said another excitedly.

"Hey you, don't you dare touch her, you have already committed a murder," teased one prisoner to another.

"And don't you dare steal the jewellery they are wearing," he replied to him.

"Shut up, you two!"

As they walked out of the hall, they were provided with different pamphlets with their timetable for the week according to their prison floor cell section.

"Each floor will have a particular activity every day!" announced the guard handing out the pamphlets.

As Ganja checked his pamphlet, he felt nothing. He had accepted whatever came his way and moved ahead for his daily wage work.

Ganja reached the ground to start his work. He was allotted the task of breaking stones with a huge hammer, one of the most difficult tasks in the jail. Only a few men who had committed grave crimes were assigned this task. As he sweated on the ground, he could see some of the women from the NGO roaming around to check on the prisoners. After their daily work, by 4 pm, it was tea time.

As Ganja sat down with his cup of tea, five women in pink approached him. A whisper spread amongst the most dangerous prisoners on seeing the pretty young woman walk across the hall and stand in the middle of the canteen. One of the women who looked the youngest announced, "Today after teatime, all of you have to assemble in the hall beside this one for your first philosophical session!" She smiled, and the women started distributing notepads and pens to all of them.

As the most horrid criminals settled in the hall, they kept grumbling and snorting, swearing under their breath for making them attend classes after such physically exhausting work. While others kept complaining to each other, giving dead stares to the guards standing there, Ganja was sitting silently, looking down at the floor, thinking of nothing, just breathing slowly, his mind at the moment, trying to be calm and composed from the exertion.

Footsteps approaching made them turn towards the gate, and the same woman with curly hair and a perfectly round face walked in wearing her light pink suit. Suddenly, the vibe of the hall changed as all 25 prisoners present turned excited upon seeing her.

"So, boys and men, how are you all?" she asked enthusiastically but only received grunting noises as a reply, while some of the young men whispered, "Good, yes, good," with a tiny smirk painted on their faces.

She smiled and said, "So, today, we will start with introductions. You will tell me your name and your crime. I will start with it. I am Madhu, and my crime is starting this NGO!" She giggled, followed by all the women standing there and some of the men in the hall. "Okay, it seems like I need to work on my humour," she sighed. So, what's your name?"

As she started asking them one by one about their family background, if any, and their crimes, she realised that most of the men in that section of the jail were rapists and sexual abusers. Some had raped their colleagues, while some had asked for a sexual compromise, abusing their positions in their companies, while some had committed the crime of indulging in marital rape.

"So, what do you think? What led you to this horrendous crime?" Madhu shot at them at once.

Some looked at her with wide eyes, while some looked awkward. Some even smiled without a pinch of shame in their eyes. The women standing as the volunteers looked at each other, seeing some of the criminals' smiles, cringed. They felt nauseous in their guts and wanted to punch those men in the faces.

"What's there to think, madam?" said one of the criminals, smiling. "We felt like doing it at that moment, so we did it with the woman before us."

"The one we could grab!" said the other, smiling and high-fiving the previous one.

While the women felt utterly disgusted and uncomfortable, Madhu's breath quickened. But she had to keep her calm and not lose her temper. With a forced smile, she said, "So you mean that if I feel like coming to you and slapping you hard on your face, I should just do it, huh?"

"No, I feel in that moment I lost the sense of right or wrong," said another who looked ashamed. "At that moment, I was angry at my girlfriend for rejecting my proposal to marry, and I really, really wanted to marry her, but she wouldn't just listen to me..." he covered his face to hide his tears. "I really miss her now. I don't understand what I have done, and how could I?" he rubbed his eyes and took deep breaths.

Hearing him feel guilty, the volunteering women looked a bit relieved. Madhu looked at him stoically and said, "I am glad at least someone has some shame," she sighed. "So now, tell me, what do you think? From where did this act come? Why couldn't you handle the rejection and force yourself upon her?"

"I don't know! I just got very angry that even after 2 years of a relationship, she was not ready to marry me. I don't understand why, and at that moment, I just felt like I wanted her, just for myself, and I wanted to do anything to make her mine. I controlled my needs for two years because, just like her, I wanted to do it after the marriage. But when she refused, I felt angry, I felt like she was betraying me. So, I wanted to make her mine, and for that, I did it right then and there."

Madhu kept looking at him with wide eyes, and all the criminals had also turned to him. Some were smiling at his story, while some felt a similar guilt. A few volunteers had misty eyes that they quietly wiped off with their handkerchiefs.

"This anger that you are repeatedly talking about," Madhu started, "Where do you think this comes from? Why can't you handle rejection?"

The man tried to think of an answer, and his face fell apart, but he couldn't think of anything. He couldn't think of a valid answer and repeated, "What made me angry?"

Madhu looked at all the prisoners. "I want you all to write down," she announced, "In whichever language you want to write, what do you feel about your crime? What do you think of yourself as a person, if human enough or not, after what you have done, and do you really want to punish yourself any longer?"

Silence fell upon the hall as they started writing, the volunteers moving from one bench to another to keep an eye on them. The silence was broken by the scribbling of the pens, sniffles, and coughs.

That night, Ganja couldn't sleep. All he kept thinking of was the woman who was raped. Her face was crying in front of him, begging him to leave her; the pain in her eyes screamed like the most helpless creature, and her tears didn't stop even for a second. And later on, she had gone silent, silent like the depths of the ocean where someone would die to hear something; their ears would screech for a voice, but there was none. Ganja sat up straight on his bed, his breath had turned shallow, and he looked into the dark nothingness. The night was the darkest, he couldn't find the moon in the sky, and all he could see from the little window in his cell was a tree whose leaves were rustling in the streetlight below.

It had been two years since Ganja was convicted for the rape of his son's girlfriend, whom his son was soon going to marry. But after the incident, the woman committed suicide, and his son went into depression. He wouldn't even come to meet his father but only go to the office, work, and come back to his mother. Ganja's wife had lost all hope of living except that she had to live for her son, make food for him, and support him to live this life. Ganja's family was going through huge debts, and if they didn't pay it on time, their house would be taken by the bank. While Ganja paid for his sins in that cell, his wife and only son tried to live for each other and pay their debts.

Only once in the past year had Ganja's wife come to meet him, and that was to get his signature on the property papers to transfer everything in the name of their son. His son was working hard, doing double shifts to pay back the debts, and the process would become easier if everything was in his name. Ganja quietly signed the papers and then tried to talk to his wife to tell her how sorry he was, but she didn't even look at him and silently walked away.

Two weeks had passed. While some continued to feel guilty, the shameless ones continued laughing and joking about what they did. But Ganja had not spoken a word about his story.

That day, Madhu and her team entered their canteen during tea time. "So, boys, today, I have decided to have tea with you all," she smiled and walked up to the stall, beaming at the staff. I'll serve them tea today," she told them, and they walked away. While Madhu prepared to pour the tea from the steel kettle into the cups, her team rearranged the tables and chairs around them to form a big round table.

As she served tea to her team and then the prisoners, they sat around the table.

"What's the plan?" asked one of the prisoners. "Why this new style of taking our class today?"

"Well, just for a change," she said, "I thought this would make you all more familiar with us, and you will be able to share your story and your thoughts with us better..." She glanced at Ganja, and he looked away. He wished not to be asked about his story again as he still wasn't ready to talk about it.

"I'll tell you mine," she said, taking glances at Ganja, and then she looked at her volunteer. "Or maybe Areena would like to tell hers?" She looked at one of her volunteers.

Areena's cup stopped midway. After a pause, she sipped the tea and placed the cup on the table. Clearing her throat, she sat up straight and looked at Madhu for courage.

Madhu nodded to her with great determination, and Areena started narrating, "I was in a relationship with my boyfriend for a year," she fidgeted with her fingers. "Our families knew each other, they liked us, and we were planning to get married," she gulped down the uneasiness as the memory flashed before her eyes. "He came to me and said, 'Marriage is a very important decision. Both the people should be happy not just emotionally but also physically.' When I looked at him confused, he cleared it by saying that…" her breath quickened, "he said that we… we should…." Areena broke down, covering her face with her palms.

Another girl sitting beside her consoled her, wrapping her hand around her, trying to calm her down when Madhu continued, "And when Areena did not listen to him, he forced himself upon her…"

There was silence. Madhu could see Ganja's eyes turning misty, but she wanted to listen to his story from his mouth and realise what he had done.

As Areena collected herself, she wiped her cheeks and said, "I couldn't take the shame. I couldn't take the pain of being raped by the love of my life. I couldn't understand how he could do that to me and how I was dumb enough to not see this coming." She paused and continued, "So, I… I wanted to end that emotional turmoil, I wanted to get rid of that shame, of that…"

The lady consoling her rubbed her thumb on her jawline and said, "The burn marks were hidden after the cosmetic surgery, but the scar on her heart is imprinted forever…"

Everyone looked at her neck carefully and realised that there were burn marks. After a more careful look at her hairline, they realised that her long voluminous hair was a wig with which she tried to hide her marks.

The guilty prisoners felt more ashamed of their acts and looked as if they wanted to evaporate into thin air and never be seen again. But the shameless ones looked unaffected by the story as if some TV serial drama was being played against their wishes.

Madhu's gut was boiling like a volcano into which she wanted to drown those audacious evildoers. She glanced at her other volunteers, and they looked firm about their plan, nodding slightly at her sight.

That night again, Ganja couldn't sleep. He couldn't help but think about Areena's distress and compare it with his situation. *How can anyone do this to someone?* He thought, and his lower lip quivered. His eyes started to pour out, and he began feeling weak.

His breath grew deeper, and his heart was beating faster. He got up from his bed and sat in the corner, taking deep breaths as he sobbed silently. His little sobs echoed in the silent hallway, and he wished no one had heard him. His heartbeat increased, and he was going breathless. He knew he needed his pump again and stood up to walk to the door of his jail. As he took a few steps, he couldn't see anything. Blinking his eyes, his head spun, and everything disappeared before him. The last thing he felt was a huge bang on his body as he shut his eyes.

"Rush everyone!" he heard faded screams. "What's going on?" Ganja tried to open his eyes and could see flashes of light. He closed them and saw pitch-dark colours throbbing in his mental sphere.

"Argh!" he felt like vomiting, and the ground below him was moving fast, as if he were on a train.

"Where am I?" he murmured in his sleep when he heard footsteps approaching. But the smell of the lady did not speak to him. Slowly, he tried to open his eyes, and he saw a well-lit room freshly painted white. He tried to move his face, but the pain in his neck and head didn't allow him to. "Where am I? Who brought me here?" he kept mumbling.

"Uncle..." he heard a voice, and slowly, he tried to move his head.

Areena's face appeared in front of him. She was misty, and Ganja couldn't understand why she looked sad. "Where am I? And..."

"You are in the government hospital near your jail..." she spoke.

"What had happened?" he groaned, his breathing increased, and he could see fog on his oxygen mask.

"You collapsed," she said with teary eyes.

"Why are you crying?" his brows narrowed.

But she did not reply. Areena kept sniffing in her handkerchief when he saw another face appear beside his bed, "Madhu madam?" He wasn't sure if he had taken the right name because his vision was blurring every few seconds.

"Good morning!" Madhu said enthusiastically.

"Good... good morning," he was confused seeing her zeal.

"Why is Areena crying?" his heart was beating fast now. "What did the doctors say?"

"Nothing," Madhu smiled. "The doctors simply said that you are in the pink of your health now. A small amount of poison was found in your body, but they have removed it."

Ganja's eyes widened on hearing this, "Poison? How? I only ate from the canteen..."

"But we were there in the canteen, weren't we?" Madhu smirked. Ganja couldn't understand her behaviour as she added, "By the way, don't you remember her?" she pointed at Areena.

Ganja's brow furrowed, and he said matter-of-factly, "She is Areena, your volunteer. "

"No, no, look at her carefully," Madhu moved Areena's hair from her wig aside so he could see her face more clearly.

Ganja kept glancing at her, confused as to why Madhu was acting strangely, and asked, "No, I don't... I don't understand... why are you asking me..."

"Look carefully..." Madhu insisted, "Take a closer look at her face..." She pulled Areena towards Ganja and bent her face lightly, "You see? You do, right?" Madhu asked aggressively.

Ganja's face moved back, "What do you mean?" he started breathing heavily, "I can't... anymore..."

"Oh, are you feeling weak now?" Madhu asked rhetorically.

"Will you please tell me... why are you..." Ganja fought for his breath; his machine started beeping as his blood pressure rose. Areena started weeping loudly and ran out of the room.

"Don't you recognise the woman you raped?" Madhu asked through gritted teeth.

Ganja's emotions suddenly turned into anger. He forgot about the confusion and the fragility he was feeling at that moment and screamed, "I did not rape! I did not..." He fought for a few more breaths as he shouted, "Did not.. rape... any... one..."

"Then why did you take the blame of a rapist? WHY?" Madhu wanted to scream louder, but she did not want to grab the staff's attention outside.

"Because I love my son!" he wept. "I couldn't see him in shackles, behind bars, I couldn't..." His eyes poured out, his lips curved down as he struggled to breathe.

His hands tried to adjust the oxygen mask, but before he could do that, Madhu held it tightly on his face. "You call this love? Setting him free after such a big heinous crime, you think you are being a good father?" she said slowly.

"No," he felt defeated, "I just did what I felt was right in that moment."

"She looked at you like her own father!" she said angrily. "Your future daughter-in-law was betrayed by her own father! Because of his blind attachment towards his son! To save a criminal son, you let your daughter burn?"

"I am… I am sorr…." He couldn't speak, his chest was heavy with guilt and regret as he realised that Areena was his future daughter-in-law whom he loved like his own, "I was shattered on finding out about… and the police came home suddenly, I did not know what to do…. I couldn't fathom the fact that my son did this!" he could speak as Madhu increased the supply of oxygen from the cylinder, and he breathed deeply, "So, in front of them, I said that not him, but I committed the crime, and he was just taking my blame…"

"Do you even realise what she must have gone through? What she must have felt in that moment standing with the police and seeing her father-like figure save her perpetrator. How dirty she must have felt in that moment? How useless, like garbage that is being thrown away, like an insect that has been stepped over! You showed her how you never loved her. And NEITHER did you love your son!" she pulled the oxygen mask, and Ganja fought for breath, "Criminals like you who try to save other rapists do not deserve to live just like rapists!" she murmured in his ears as his palms slapped on her hand, trying to put the mask back. But Ganja was weak, and she was very strong.

He couldn't move her arm, and he joined his palms to plead with her, "Please…" he hissed, his eyes widened, and his legs banging on the bed.

Chapter 6

The Contemplation

The café was silent, seeing Inspector Rithika sitting at the middle table with a glass of whisky in one hand and munching on chickpeas in the other. The waiters stood there in attention, ready to move at once upon receiving any orders from her. Half of the customers had left the shady café, which was situated in the corner of a small market, and the rest were big-time criminals who were aware of the laws.

"Why are you scared?" a fat man scoffed in a white shirt and white pants. "She cannot do anything until she catches us red-handed," he patted his younger brother, who now looked calmer.

"She looks wasted!" whispered the younger brother.

"None of our business," the fat man chugged his beer as he saw another empty table. The more customers entered the café, the more they left upon seeing her there.

"Sir," whispered the junior staff to his manager, "Four customers have already left; today our business will fail because a police inspector is our customer!"

The manager caressed his beard, "I know, I was thinking the same, we really need to do something!" he said through gritted teeth as he saw Rithika raise her arm and call the waiter to refill her glass. He slowly walked up to her and inspected her table to understand why the inspector had come to his criminal-infused shady café out of all the high society reputed cafes in the city. He smiled at her and acted as if asking her for anything else that she needed, but Rithika just nodded with her eyes half-shut. The manager stood there defeated, furrowing his brows when his attention was caught by her phone flashing, "Insp Muthu"

Rithika clicked her tongue as she cancelled the call and threw a chickpea in her mouth when her phone beeped again. Without looking at her phone, she silenced the call by pressing the power button on the side.

The manager grew impatient. He wanted her to pick up her phone and go to her duty or anywhere just out of this café. But as he realised she was avoiding the call, he had an idea. He picked up the tray from the hands of the staff and went to her table. He picked up the used glass and slowly wiped the table when her phone rang. As Rithika was chugging down another glass, he pressed the answer button and asked Rithika loudly, "Ma'am, I hope you love our services at the Hedon Café And Bar!" He smirked at her.

Rithika groaned irritably, "Where is my biryani? I ordered it an hour ago!"

He looked at the phone that the caller had cancelled and smirked, "Yes, it must be on the way."

The manager had to wait impatiently for another ten to fifteen minutes when he finally saw a well-dressed and heavily built man enter their bar and walk straight up to Rithika. "Inspector Rithika!" he said, taking a seat beside her. The manager sighed with relief, looking at his staff and gesturing to him that he would now take her away.

"What is wrong with you?" Inspector Muthuswamy asked her as he looked at her dishevelled state. "Why can't you..." He held her wrist and snatched the glass away from her.

"Don't you dare!" she said. "Leave me!"

The manager sent the bill to the staff by doubling all the rates for the losses they had incurred that night.

Muthuswamy looked at the bill for 4,000 rupees, retrieved two notes for 2,000 rupees from his wallet, and then pulled Rithika off the table. "Please come with me. We need to talk…"

Reluctantly, she walked out with him, tripping and colliding with other tables on her way.

"What is wrong with you, Rithika? I have been calling you since morning!" Muthuswamy murmured as he helped her inside his car. In all the chaos of picking her up and making her walk to the car, her shirt had shifted up to her chest. Muthuswamy could see her wheatish waist. His hands reached her shirt to pull it down and cover her up as he got up at once and closed the door.

It had started raining, and he quickly got on the wheels and drove off, "Why did you go to that café from where you always wanted to catch every criminal?"

Rithika didn't answer. She kept murmuring about how she wanted to end the evil in the world, and he sneered at her with adoration in his eyes. They stopped at a signal, and he looked at her dozing beside him. Her hair was messed up, and a strand fell on her face, tickling her lips.

Muthuswamy felt uncomfortable because he wanted to tuck the strand behind her ears, but he was also scared of doing so. *"Touching her is dangerous, she can wake up from her drunkard state and start kicking my butt!"* he thought to himself and chuckled internally.

The traffic did not recede, and there was chaos on the street. The cars were honking uncontrollably when Muthuswamy turned on the news and put on his earphones, "There is a possibility of a cloudburst tonight. It is advisable to remain indoors and not travel anywhere as per the weather forecast."

He tapped his fingers on the steering wheel, and after much thought, he turned the car around and did the unthinkable.

*** * ***

The next afternoon, Rithika woke up with a throbbing headache. She couldn't open her eyes because of the pain and just sat upright for a couple of minutes. As she opened her eyes slowly, she looked around and was confused. Quickly, she looked down, but she was in her clothes from the previous night, "Where am I?" she whispered to herself. That's when she heard a knock on the door, and she covered herself with the blanket.

The doorknob turned, and a lady entered the room with a tray, "Oh, you have woken up!" she asked with a smile and kept the tray on the bedside, "I'll call for Saab," she said and walked away.

Rithika checked the tray that had a hot glass of water with honey and a pain reliever spray.

Again, there was a knock, and Muthuswamy entered with a smile, "I hope you had a good night's sleep," he looked awkward, "Umm, I know what you must be thinking… actually, it was raining heavily, and the forecast said it is dangerous to travel, and your house was far away from where you chose to get drunk…" he pursed his mouth. Rithika nodded understandingly and murmured a thank you, "Get ready, I have asked my maid to keep the essentials in the bathroom for your use," he said.

There was silence as they sat. Rithika felt awkward at his genuine care towards her and wanted to leave right away. But as she tried to get up from her bed, her throbbing head didn't let her stand straight, and she fell back onto her bed.

"Rithi…" Muthuswamy held her by her waist, standing on his knee on the bed, he said softly, "Be careful…"

"My head is throbbing," she whispered, holding her forehead, and Muthuswamy helped her to sit back. Slowly and reluctantly, she picked up the glass of honey water and drank it.

"You freshen up," he said and left.

Rithika nodded. Applying the spray to her forehead, she took a deep breath and went inside the bathroom to freshen up.

An hour later, she walked out of the room and saw Muthuswamy reading his newspaper at the dining table. "Ah! Finally, you are here. Let's have our lunch," he said, folding his paper and keeping it aside.

"Haven't you had your lunch yet?" she asked.

"No ma'am, I couldn't have it without my guest," he gestured to his maid to bring in the food.

Rithika smiled, "Intruder, I'll say..."

"Well, I guess I am glad this intruder chose my place," he beamed at her, and the maid brought in two plates of biryani.

After the meal, Rithika tried to put herself together and shed her embarrassment as she started, "Listen, I... I know I was a mess... a chaos yesterday... and... I am sorry that you had to... but... thank you so much... but you... Muthu, you really didn't have to... I mean I know I was..."

"Rithika, I have always considered you a good friend even though I know we have our little quarrels and disagreements... So, I guess I could do so much for my friend..."

Rithika looked at him with misty eyes and nodded. She quickly blinked her eyes to prevent them from flowing and said, "I was suspended yesterday..."

"I know..."

"But I cannot shrug off the fact that they caught someone else for the murder of..."

"I know, that is what you have been murmuring on our way here in the car…" Rithika felt more embarrassed as he added, "I think I totally understand where you are coming from and what you are feeling about this case. We are police officers who regularly see the insensitive and cruel side of the world, but in some cases, they do not let us be the tough people that we become in our profession. In some cases, we do take them to heart, and we want to solve them anyhow," as he peered into her eyes, she nodded and he said, "So stop being so embarrassed in front of me, and you know I am with you."

"But I am suspended, how will I…"

"I am not. You do the groundwork, and I will search for the files at the office whenever required. We will find the culprit or the gang, whoever is behind these murders." Rithika nodded as he added, "And please, I would prefer the badass Rithika who would show me my place at every word I say, not the one embarrassed on being suspended or found drunk at a bar."

Rithika sighed, "More than that, I am utterly disappointed, Muthu, our IG whom I looked up to, who wasn't corrupt, and I understand he isn't. It is just that he was under the pressure of being transferred because of which he had to listen to the political leaders and…" she took a deep breath. "I am not so much embarrassed by what I did but by the system that doesn't let us be honest and seek justice for everyone." Her lower lip trembled. "We are all in a state of war against each other!"

Muthu gently placed his hand on her shoulder and said, "Chill, not everyone is like that. There are people like you and me who are ready to fight against the wrong in the right way."

She covered her face with her palms and rubbed it vigorously. Taking a deep breath, she asked, "What's the plan?" and looked at him with determination.

Muthu smiled at her and said, "Now you are talking!" He walked up to his desk and retrieved a file from the drawer. Sitting back at the table beside Rithika, he opened the file and said, "As I had researched, we had these murders in the past couple of months committed on rapists. Fingers were chopped off from the victims of killings in Chennai, Mohali, and UP. All of them had rape charges against them in the past couple of years but were roaming freely. Then, an old man was tortured for a month and then finally killed in Darjeeling, in the same manner, that he had tortured and raped a little girl," He showed the newspaper clippings of his news, "And this is his case file."

"Why was he not convicted?" she asked, checking his complaint report.

"He was, but he was out on bail. He was a rich landlord and had no family except some trustworthy friends in the area whom he owed a lot of favours, and hence they helped him get bail," he passed her another file, "And this is the file of the four men who were burnt in an already burnt house in Mandi. According to the DNA reports, they were the same men who were convicted for the rape of a minor girl on their vacation in Mandi. They were then burnt in the same house where the minor girl lived with her parents and where the family had committed suicide."

"The Monster House!" Rithika read the news from Mandi. "This is the house where a beautiful family lived and burnt themselves alive when their daughter was found raped. In this same monster house, four men were found burnt. What does this house want? Why has it turned into a hell on earth?" Rithika's brows furrowed as she turned to Muthuswamy and said, "What is wrong with the media houses? They are blaming the acts of humans on a HOUSE?"

Her nose wrinkled, and a strand of hair fell on her face as Muthuswamy kept staring at her, her breath slowly exhaling when she asked, "Yes?"

"Huh?" he said, emerging from his dream. "Yes, it makes us feel better by saying that the house or the thing is impure or corrupt, not the human," Muthu shrugged. We leave no chance of blaming things that make us feel less guilty of being this species called humans."

Rithika kept staring at all the newspaper clippings and their reports. She tried connecting the dots and said, "A man killed the same way as he raped the girl. Four men were killed in the same way as their victims' families ended. And fingers? Why were they chopped....."

"They were internet abusers. They morphed the women's pictures and videos into sexual ones," he explained.

"So, they chopped their fingers that they used for this sin..." Rithika sighed, and Muthusway nodded at her. "So, we can conclude that all these recent murders of rapists could be done by the same person."

"Or a gang,"

"Someone who is avenging the rape of all these girls, someone whose mother, sister, or daughter was once raped, I guess, or someone who is too affected by the rapes in the country."

"Exactly!"

She blew air sharply from her nose.

After a few seconds of silence, as she grappled with the information, she finally said, "So, now, our next step would be to find all those rapists who are roaming free in the country."

"Yes... the gang's next target would be one of them, and we will have to keep an eye on them," he said.

"And just when the gang catches any of these previously convicted sexual abusers, we will be able to follow them and catch them..."

"Yes…but…"

"But which city should we start from?"

"Exactly my concern…"

Rithika thought deeply, "They do not have a pattern as of now. Or maybe, they are randomly catching hold of people from various cities wherever they can."

"We can start from here itself, in Chennai, and find all those abusers," he said. "We have no other option but to wait. Wait for the gang to attack someone in this city."

Rithika nodded, "We should send this data all over the country and tell the officers in each jurisdiction to be aware of a previous rape convict being murdered. We will have to ask them to inform us about any killing that takes place and where the victim was a criminal himself."

"I'll get on to it," Muthuswamy nodded and got up to leave.

"Also, I'll need the file of rape convicts," she said.

"I'll bring that file home, and you can use this whiteboard for further research and study while I connect with the officers pan India," he said and left.

By evening, Muthuswamy came home with a big fat file clutched in his arms, "This contains all the FIRs for rape and molestation charges of the past two years. The report attached to it will tell us if they are convicted or not."

Rithika took the file from him eagerly and started checking each FIR thoroughly. Muthuswamy went inside to freshen up when he saw the whiteboard full of markings. Rithika had written about the recent cases and their details, trying to connect any dots between them. An hour later, the doorbell rang, and two officers entered the house.

"Ah! Finally, you've arrived!" Muthuswamy welcomed the constables. Rithika looked confused, and he explained to her, "They'll help us with the case, unofficially."

"Why unofficially?" her brow narrowed.

"Because it is your case," the constable explained, "and you are sus..." he pursed his lips.

"But only for a week, then she'll be back!" Muthuswamy challenged the constable. "Then see what will happen to you!" he smirked at him.

"No, ma'am, I am here for you, and for this mysterious case, I really want to…" he said with fear in his voice.

Rithika giggled, "He is just teasing you, Bablu. I am glad that you are here," she smiled, and he looked relieved.

All night, the officers sifted through the reports of the rapists who had not been jailed or even caught and those who had been caught and imprisoned but were then out on bail.

The constables attended calls with the officers who replied to Rithika's email that she had prepared in the afternoon after Muthuswamy had left. The officers from all over the country wanted to understand the situation in depth and their further plan of action. Bablu and Bhola explained their ideas as instructed by Rithika to talk on the call.

It was dawn when they were ready with the list of non-convicted sexual abusers in Chennai. After having dinner prepared by Muthuswamy's maid, they all slept on their tables and couches.

✳ ✳ ✳

Kaali was on his way to his hotel. For a few days, he was on time, doing his chores on time and reporting to his manager sincerely. He was in debt for what his manager had done for him, and he wanted to be his perfect staff. Right as he reached the hotel, he greeted his manager and started the work 10 minutes earlier than his reporting time.

The manager glared at him and dropped his glass of water. He then clicked his fingers and gestured for Kaali to clean it up. With a smile, Kaali wiped the floor and said, "I will always be in your debt, sir."

The manager scoffed, "Why do you think I did what I did to save you? It was only to save the image of our hotel. Not for you!" Kaali nodded and walked away.

* * *

Rithika woke up after three hours. She made coffee for all four of them and woke them up, "We have had our rest, guys, now it is time for action."

Muthuswamy called for more constables and emailed them the list for their respective jurisdictions. He then called them up individually and said, "Good morning, sir! We are on a mission to safeguard the non-convicted sexual abusers because there is a gang that is murdering them. As per the recent crimes, many such abusers who are roaming free were killed brutally and in the same manner as they killed or left their victims in a horrific state." After explaining to them in detail about all the recent events, he said, "So, we are mailing you the list of such abusers who are at the risk of being attacked by the gang. They live in your jurisdiction, and we want you to contact them, warn them, and keep an eye on them for any strange action in their life. As soon as you find anything weird, contact us immediately and we will be on our way."

Rithika and Bablu went on their way to meet and talk to the abusers in their jurisdiction when Bablu said, "I can't believe that we are working to protect such abusers!" His brows furrowed.

"I understand, but when someone takes the law into their hands, the law has to bend a little to protect itself from being exploited," Rithika explained, and Bablu nodded.

* * *

The manager called Kaali and said, "There is a new guest, go and help them with their luggage."

Kaali reached the reception at once and saw a lady with curly hair and dusky skin, standing with her red suitcase. She smiled at him, and he picked up her luggage. "Room no. 705," the manager said, and Kaali went straight to the lift, followed by the lady.

* * *

Three days had passed, but Rithika and her team hadn't received even a small piece of information from any of the jurisdictions in the city of Chennai. They kept in touch with the abusers; some rich ones even bought a few officers to stand outside their houses 24/7. While some powerful ones dared to talk rudely with the seniors, "I don't understand what your force is doing. How come I am under the threat of being killed for a mistake I committed half a decade ago?" Rithika's blood boiled on hearing this. But she had no other option than to listen to everything to be able to find the gang.

* * *

Kaali was asked to collect a parcel by the new guest at the hotel. The address that she gave was in a small lane at the far corner of the city. She paid him well enough to do the work by taking leave from his official duty.

She befriended him quite well in the previous three days of her stay. She would always ask him about his health, family, and education. She would teach him about better financing ways to help his family, and Kaali felt seen and blessed. So, Kaali couldn't say no to her and took leave from the hotel, saying, "My mother is suddenly ill; I need to take her to the doctor."

As he was going, he couldn't stop thinking about the new guest. Her beautiful smile and her big eyes. Her sweet voice whenever she had a conversation with him. Kaali made sure to go to her room for cleaning service and any other assistance that she required. He felt good after a long time when someone treated him so well.

As he reached the lane, he checked the address and searched for the house. It was in the far corner of the lane and had a dilapidated building. As Kaali stepped inside the house, his heart skipped a beat.

* * *

Rithika was getting impatient. Her suspension from duty had left her with very little to do for the case. She couldn't find the culprits on her own. She had to wait for another four days for her suspension to be over. In frustration, she banged her fist on the table and called the officers for updates.

As soon as Kaali entered the house, he was greeted by two women who handed him a parcel with a smile. When he turned around, he saw another lady close the door and lock it. Kaali was confused. He couldn't understand that move. But seeing only women inside, he did not fear anything. "What happened? I have to give this parcel to the woman staying at our hotel, right?" he asked.

"Who said that?" asked one of the ladies.

"Mam said to collect the parcel from this address," his throat turned dry.

"Yes, so you have collected it, right?" said another lady sweetly. "Where did she mention that the parcel was for her?"

Kaali's brows furrowed, and his eyes narrowed, "I don't understand..."

"Open the parcel, Kaali, it is for you," she said, and he was stunned that she knew his name. Not even the madam at the hotel had asked for his name, but this lady knew it, how?

Anyhow, Kaali opened the box and found another box inside, a small one. As he opened it, he saw two pairs of hearing aid machines, one of which was broken. Kaali's eyes widened on seeing it. He couldn't believe what he was seeing, "How? How do you have this?" he stuttered.

"So, I am guessing that you remember very well what this is and, most importantly, WHOSE this is," said the lady.

"See, let me go. I don't want to be here. My manager must be waiting for me," he said as he took a few steps back.

"But you told him your mother is not well, and you need a day off, right? So why would he wait for you?"

Kaali turned around and ran towards the door, banging on it and screaming, "Somebody open up the door, please!" His face started sweating as he tried to escape and look for another way to escape, but he couldn't find one. One by one, the ladies came out of the rooms of that house, and he saw so many women surround him. Fear was gripping him from top to bottom when he saw the wicked smiles on their faces.

"I beg of you, it was a mistake, I didn't really. I am sorry, please let me go, I swear I will go to the police and give myself up. But please leave me."

* * *

Two days had passed, and Rithika knew that she would be able to do something about the situation only after she was back to her duty. That day, Muthuswamy came home running and told her, "There is a police complaint of a missing person."

Rithika got up with hope as Muthuswamy informed her, "A hotel staff is missing for two days. He had said that his mother was ill and that's why he needed a leave. But for two days, the manager was not able to contact him," as he continued to inform her, Rithika collected her gun and other essentials to get ready to leave, "Other staff who know him closely also haven't heard from him. So, they have filed a missing report," he paused. Rithika looked at him with hope in her eyes, waiting for the main news, and he said,

"As per our case file reports, that missing man had molested a girl when she had come to stay at their hotel a year ago."

Rithika exhaled deeply and asked impatiently, "So, did he kill her or traumatise her? I am sure the gang will do the same with him."

"He didn't. This time, the abuser did not leave her in a pathetic condition."

"So, what do you think the gang is going to do with him and where?"

"As per the reports," he placed the file on the table, and she opened it, "He entered her room to clean but then found the opportunity to touch her inappropriately a few times. As she pushed him and started screaming, he ran out of the room and left the floor silently. The woman complained about him later to the manager and also called the police. But the manager said that the staff wasn't there as he had sent him out for some work. He showed a bill as proof, and even the CCTV was not working on that floor that day. The police concluded that due to the cameras not working, the staff must have taken advantage of it. Due to a lack of evidence, after spending some time in the locker, the police had to allow him to be bailed by the manager who wanted to save the face of the hotel's name. The manager then told the media that the lady must have mistaken him for someone else, most probably a guest."

As Muthuswamy paused, Rithika stared at him and said, "And the media, did the people accept such a dumb explanation by the manager?"

"The owner of the hotel interfered, saying that..." Muthu's throat dried as he looked down at the floor and added, "That the girl was deaf and dumb, her normal speech sounds like a... a scream sometimes, so her eyes could also have been..."

Rithika's gut feeling turned into a volcano,

"Could her eyes also have been?"

"Have been... mistaken... seeing the... person..."

"Aargh!" Rithika screamed from the depths of her lungs.

Muthuswamy stood there frozen, letting her let out her anger so that she felt lighter during work. He wanted to hold her and caress her. He wanted to be there for her, but he couldn't. He was a colleague.

Rithika couldn't fathom the fact that to save the name of a brand, some people could let a woman live with the trauma of having been molested without any justice. And on top of that, blame her disability. Her eyes watered as she again contemplated going after the gang. In one corner of her heart, she strongly felt that she should let the gang do whatever they wished with the convict and asked, "Is the gang right in doing what they are doing?" she asked Muthuswamy with a pinch of shame for questioning her uniform.

"Their intentions must be good, but their ways are not. And who knows, tomorrow their information may not be correct, and they kill an innocent person?" he kept his palm on her shoulder. "Come on, be strong, and we will catch this person before the gang kills him this time," he said, and she nodded at him with determination.

"Let's go!" she said, tucking her revolver into the back of her jeans and rushed out.

Rithika got into the car, and Muthuswamy drove her to the hotel. On the way, she called Bablu and Bambi, their constables, and asked them to reach the hotel.

"So, what time did Kaali leave the hotel that day?" Rithika asked the manager after listening to his side of the story.

"Around 11 a.m.," the manager replied.

"So, it has been 3 days exactly since you or any of the staff saw him," she said as she walked in the reception area. "Are you sure that your staff, this Kaali, has not committed any crime since his last molestation case?" she glared into the manager's eyes.

"No, I am sure he hasn't," the manager looked uncomfortable.

"How can you be so sure? Why do you trust him so much?" she asked.

"I have known him for many years now. He felt very guilty after his mistake last time. So, when I..."

"His mistake?" Rithika asked firmly. "Can you kindly repeat to me what his mistake was?"

"Uh, he... uh... molested a girl and..."

"And that you call a mistake? Is it just a mistake?" Her face was scowling from every corner.

"No, I mean, yeah, what else... I mean, I didn't..." the manager held his breath in fear.

"Molestation is NOT a MISTAKE!" she spat at him. "It is a SIN! A CRIME!" she screamed at the top of her lungs.

"Ye-ss-s, yes, ma'am," the manager nodded.

"Did you check at his place?" Muthuswamy asked.

"Yes, sir," the manager replied. "One of our staff lives near his house, and they come together sometimes."

"Who is he?" Muthuswamy asked.

The concerned staff stepped in front and said, "It is I, sir."

"What did you find at his place when you met him?" Muthuswamy asked.

"Sir, he was not there. His mother was not ill. She was fine. She said that he hadn't come for 3 days. The last time she saw him was when he left for work early in the morning that day."

Rithika was stunned by his revelation. She turned around and instructed her constable, "I need every detail related to the woman he molested a year ago. And if possible, bring her to the police station. I need to talk to her..." She walked away, followed by Muthuswamy.

Outside their car, Rithika looked worried. "I am sure they have already kidnapped Kaali. They must have even murdered him. Or God knows what else they would have done to him. They are ahead of us, Muthu, they are…" Rithika was on the verge of breaking down.

He touched her shoulders and said, "Don't worry, we will find him!" With his thumb, he wiped a tear from the corner of her eye.

Chapter 7

Desire Turns Deaf and Dumb

It was the last day of Rithika's suspension. She was on her way to the police station. As Muthuswamy drove the jeep, he asked, "Why do you look worried? Now we have proof to show the IG. He will have to listen to us now and reopen the case officially."

"What proof do we have?" Rithika said nonchalantly.

"Once again, a non-convicted sexual abuser is missing. It adds to your chain of evidence."

"But for that, we will need to find him and find out if he was really abducted by the gang or if he was missing due to some other reason."

"We will find out, don't worry," Muthuswamy said. His palm reached for her hand as he was about to place it above hers but then stopped. He slowly took his hand back and sighed with relief because Rithika was looking out of the window.

They approached the main road and were just about to reach the police station when they got stuck in traffic.

HONK! HONK!

The cars were honking impatiently, and the signal looked far away. "The traffic is immense! Seems like there is an accident or something."

"I'll call Bablu and ask him to take another route," Rithika picked up her phone when there was a knock on her window.

TAP TAP

"Hey! Get out of here," Muthuswamy called out to the beggar and gestured for him to go away with his palm.

"Hello, Bablu?" Rithika said on the call.

KNOCK KNOCK!

The beggar banged again, and Rithika looked at him. "There is too much traffic here," she told Bablu on the call and saw the beggar spreading his palm, asking for money. When she told Bablu, "Go from another route."

Muthuswamy rolled down the window. "Didn't you understand? Don't trouble us!" he said loudly to the beggar.

The beggar's eyes were closed, and he was weeping uncontrollably. He mumbled as he cried out, "O FOO, Hungyyy, Wawa…HAP!"

Rithika's brow narrowed as she held her forehead and exhaled deeply.

Muthuswamy rolled up the windows and stepped on the accelerator. The signal seemed to have turned green as all the vehicles were moving further, and he said, "I have seen so many disabled people work hard these days. Be it starting their own business or selling on the streets. In fact, the government has come up with so many rules to support them. But some people… they only want sympathy for their disability." Rithika sighed. Her eyes were glued to the signal that now showed 110 seconds to go. Muthuswamy looked at her. He could see the worry on her forehead and the hopelessness in her eyes. So, he tried to continue with the conversation, "Now look at that beggar," he pointed at a woman, "She looks perfectly healthy. In fact, she is carrying a baby with so much ease, so she must be strong too. Can she not work?" Rithika nodded, and Muthuswamy saw the blind beggar come back and knock on his side of the window, "He is back! God help us!" he shook his head, "I'll give him some coins," Muthuswamy pulled the window glass down and said in the local language, "Please move aside, otherwise you'll get hurt when I drive." He said, waving his hand at the beggar to go away after placing money in his palm.

But the beggar kept mumbling unclear words, "O-Oh, HAP… HAP! Ooeesss…"

The beggar stuck out his tongue, and Muthuswamy cringed at him. He quickly rolled the window, saying, "Are you deaf?" The signal turned green, and he drove off, cringing a little. "The beggar's tongue was cut; God knows what he did with it."

"Why would he cut his own tongue?" Rithika finally said something after a long time.

"Oh, yeah," Muthu chuckled, "That was dumb of me, why would he…"

Rithika looked at him with wide eyes. "Stop the car!" Muthuswamy turned the wheel to take the car aside and pressed the brakes at once. That beggar! His tongue was cut, and he was possibly deaf," she said loudly and got out of the car. Muthuswamy tried to digest what she had just said and got out of the car.

Rithika was running through the traffic and between the vehicles as they honked at her loudly. But she did not pay heed to any of the drivers, "Hey, hey, what are you up to?" screamed a man from his car.

"Rithika!" Muthu yelled at her, chasing behind her. But she kept running towards the beggar, searching for him hastily.

Rithika hadn't looked at the beggar when he had come to her window. She didn't pay attention to him other than just glancing at him to remember his dark complexion, short height, and round face.

Her breath was rapid as she looked around at the vehicles zooming through the green signal. Her hand was pulled with force as she was taken to the divider of the road, "What is wrong with you?" Muthu screamed at her, "Why are you running on the main road with hundreds of cars around you?"

"Muthu-mu…" she tried to catch her breath, but Rithika kept panting, "It could have been him!"

He shouted, "Who?"

"The beggar!"

"What?"

"The beggar was deaf, and his tongue was wounded!" she looked around at the beggars gathered on the footpath and tried to cross the road.

But Muthuswamy held her arm, "I do not understand, Rithika, what are you...?"

"They did not kill him!" she howled. "They made him deaf and mute like the girl he molested!"

The signal turned red again, and the cars stopped. Zooming in between them, Rithika reached the beggars on the footpath who had started to scatter away to beg from the cars.

She looked around for the poor man, and so did Muthuswamy, when her phone rang. She picked it up in haste, "Hello? Ma'am? We have reached. Where are you?"

"Not now, Bablu, I'll call you..." she hung up and wiped her forehead. Her face was sweating profusely, and her vision was blurring in the heat.

"Hey, we are going to find that man!" Muthuswamy assured her as he started asking the other beggars around, "Hey, do you know that deaf and mute beggar?"

"He was new, and this is our area!" shouted a beggar.

"We kicked him out of here; he cannot beg here in our area!" said the lady with the child.

Muthu pulled his hair, "Where did he go?" he asked them.

"How would we know?" the beggars said and walked away.

"What happened? I couldn't find him anywhere!" Rithika said, panting.

Muthuswamy had no reply. He looked around at all the beggars on the road and said, "He's gone..."

Rithika picked up her phone, "Hello, Bablu! Come to HP main road at the signal, NOW!"

* * *

"Ahh! Help me!" the mute beggar screamed as his mouth was covered with a cloth and he was pulled into a van.

"So, you were trying to act smart, huh?" said a lady holding his neck under her biceps. "Trying to talk to the police, huh?" she said through clenched teeth.

The beggar could see that he was inside a vehicle, away from the main road. He could see huge trees around him, and there was a calmness in the surroundings compared to the main road where he begged. "Wheew am I? Aahh!! " He started weeping and crying. "Eeaase eeww mee!" He joined his hands to plead to her.

"Leave you, huh?" she threw him away and he fell under the seat as the van started, "Aarghh! Wheew ain mee?""

"Wheew aainn aainn!" another lady in the car mimicked him teasingly, "Why are you screaming like a retard?"

"Oh, no, Sujata. He is not screaming; he is pleading to leave him," said the man with a big muscular body.

"Oh!" Sujata exclaimed. "Just like that deaf girl pleaded, but they said her words are near to a scream?"

Kaali bawled under the seat. He did not even get up from there. He wanted to remain cramped up in the corner as he was now scared of the women. He was scared of what more they planned to do with him like they had done two days back. They threw the parcel from his hands, tied him up to a chair, and tied his mouth with a rope so tight that it pained his jaw. Then they inserted hot iron sticks in his ears as he screamed and howled for life, but the tied rope suppressed it. His eyes watered like an ocean as he couldn't breathe anymore, and he stopped panting. Slowly the next moment, a woman removed his rope, and he saw the bodybuilder approaching him with a blade. A blade he saw kept in the fire before him was now reaching his mouth. The lady held his jaw so tightly that he couldn't move. His hands and legs were already tied up with a rope, and he restlessly moved and shivered, "NOOO!! PLEASE!!" were his last words as the lady held his tongue and wounded it severely, his eyes closed, and his mind stopped.

* * *

"Ma'am!" Rithika heard Bablu's voice and turned around. She saw him and Bambi reach her with quick steps and ushered them to run to her.

"Hear me out!" Rithika said impatiently. "I saw a beggar here who had his tongue wounded as if to make him dumb, and he seemed deaf too," she looked at the constables and continued, "So I really want to meet him and talk to him just to be sure if he is…"

"Kaali?" both the constables said in unison.

Rithika nodded and told them about his present condition: "Right now, he is not seen here. God knows where he has gone. But I want to wait here for him, and we need to catch him anyway!"

"Yes, ma'am!" they said again in unison.

"But Rithika, we can go to the police station to talk to the IG," Muthuswamy said. "If he believes us and decides to help us, we will get official orders to carry out this search and..."

"No, Muthuswamy," Rithika glared at the beggars, "I don't want to go without evidence. I will meet the IG with Kaali, who can be the witness to what I said that day."

* * *

The next moment when Kaali woke up, it was dark around, and he couldn't hear anything. He was lying on the floor, in the mud, and was scared that they made him blind, too. But then he saw a ray of light coming right at him, and he blinked his eyes for a better view. As he opened and closed his eyes, he spoke, "Who are they?" and his tongue pinged like he had screws inside his mouth, "Aarrghh!" he wept again.

"Come and have your food," said the heavy voice of a lady.

"Whaaa??" he sobbed as his world had turned silent, and the lady picked him up by his collar as if he were a dirty animal and brought him out. She threw him on the ground, and Kaali wiped his eyes and mouth to look around.

A fire was burning in the centre, and many women sat there and surrounded it. They were having their food when Kaali's eyeballs fixed on a familiar lady. She was looking at him with clenched fists; her breathing was rapid, and there were tears in her eyes.

The bodybuilder lady pulled him by his collar to drag him up to the lady he was looking at. Kaali's heartbeat increased as he kept staring at the familiar lady.

"What happened? You still haven't recognised her as what?" asked another woman even though she knew he couldn't hear her. She walked in front of him and Kaali's eyes widened on seeing the same dusky girl with curly hair that he served at his hotel for two days. His lower lip trembled, and his vision blurred as he tried to speak, but his tongue could only say, "Ma'am… eease eave meee!" he joined his hands.

"What is he babbling?" the dusky girl cringed.

"He is just screaming because he is dumb," said another lady. "So, we should have caught the boss too!"

"Yes, the boss said that but for whom?" the dusky girl shouted, "Whom did he want to save for the sake of his name? This filth! This Kaali who molested that innocent little girl!" she pointed at the lady sitting in front of him with clenched fists, "She did not get justice then. But now, seeing him suffer like her, live her life of a dumb and mute," she whispered her last words at him as if casting a spell on him to curse him, "you are going to go through worse!"

* * *

The van was running over the potholes while Kaali still sat cramped up under the seat. The ladies took him to the signal and wrote a message for him to read. Kaali held the paper with his shaky fingers and read in his mind, "*We will always keep our eyes on you. Don't you dare try to talk to any police officer or else… you will lose your life too!*"

Kaali walked up to the divider and looked at both sides. On one side, he could see the beggars frowning at him, asking him to go away as this was their locality to beg. On the other side, the women who would kill him. He had no option but to listen to the women. He had acceptance in this world. And looking at his condition, he knew he would not be accepted by the society where he came from. While on the other side, the women wanted him to live a life full of hell and disrespect. He had no voice, no sound. He was over. There was no hope of the future. He couldn't do anything to survive. And he couldn't show his face to his mother anymore.

The gang of women would make sure that he paid for his sins all his life. Something that he thought he would pay after his death, in the kingdom of God. But he had forgotten that one has to pay for their sins on this planet itself. Kaali didn't see a life ahead. He only saw hell. And that, he was ready to see after reaching the end of the realms only.

The signal turned green, and Kaali looked at the cars zooming away. His heart was pounding like drums in his chest, and he wanted to end this pain.

Rithika and Muthuswamy were standing on the other side of the road, observing the beggars at the far end to see if any of them were deaf or dumb. Bablu and Bambi had gone on a tea break after two hours of waiting and searching for Kaali.

Kaali kept his feet steady when he saw a huge black sedan speeding towards him. His heart was beating faster, and his breathing became rapid as he took another step towards the car.

Muthuswamy looked around, away from the troop of beggars when he saw another poor man standing a little away from the divider, looking at the speeding cars coming in his direction. He then observed the beggar again and realised that he was the one they were searching for, "Rithika!" he said loudly only for her to hear him, and she looked at him.

Rithika peered in the direction of his eyesight and saw the beggar taking another step to reach the middle of the road. Just as the sedan was about to reach him, Rithika ran towards him screaming, "No! Kaali!"

Muthuswamy saw her running towards Kaali and caught up with her speed, "Wait! Rithika!"

The beggars on the other side heard the chaos and watched the scene with wide eyes. "Aaarghh!" screamed the lady with a baby in her arms, covering her eyes.

Bablu and Bambi had just returned from their break and yelled in unison, "Madam!"

Rithika was storming towards Kaali in the middle of the road, screaming, "Kaali! Don't do this!"

"Stop!" Muthuswamy bellowed from behind and reached her just as the sedan touched Kaali.

"Aahh!" Rithika roared as she held Kaali by his arms and fell on the road. Muthuswamy crashed with the sedan whose driver had pressed on the brakes at once upon seeing the lady run towards them. The car skidded ahead, and Muthuswamy hung on its bonnet. Bablu ran towards Muthuswamy to help him as the car stopped, while Bambi ran up to Rithika to make sure that she was fine.

Chapter 8

Kaali And Maa

Rithika's head was throbbing with pain as the nurse applied medicine to her forehead and tied a bandage around it.

"Please look here," the nurse held her chin and moved her face in front of her. But Rithika was continuously peering at Kaali. She wanted to make sure that he would not run away even though he was handcuffed and had the constable guarding him. She had played with her life to protect him as she jumped over to him in the middle of the road. Kaali and Rithika fell on the divider, Rithika's head banging on the stone while Kaali fell straight on the divider, injuring his back.

As the other nurse tied a crepe bandage around Kaali's back and abdomen, she informed them and the other constables standing there, "He doesn't have a fracture, but let's wait for the X-ray reports. If there is even a minor crack, we'll have to treat it. It's the spine after all," she picked up her tray and walked away.

Rithika stood up from her bed and walked up to Kaali. She stared at him, glancing from top to bottom, her brows furrowed. But then her head throbbed again, her eyes closed, and she was about to lose her balance when

Muthuswamy held her from behind, "Watch it! Here…" Holding her arms, he helped her to sit on the chair beside her. Rithika held her forehead and let out a sigh. Looking at her, Muthuswamy said, "You need rest for a day at least…"

"No!" Rithika said at once and looked at Kaali. "He is our only hope to take this case ahead. I cannot wait to investigate and question him. The IG should know that there is definitely a gang behind…"

"He can know everything tomorrow, Rithika," Muthuswamy said firmly, "But for that, you will need to be perfectly fine."

Just then, Rithika's parents entered the room where they were being treated.

"*Aiyoo*! Rithikaa…" her mom exclaimed.

"*Amma*, it's all fine, please don't overrea…" she groaned as her mother started caressing her head.

"What happened on the field?" her father asked her and looked at Kaali with suspicion. "Is he the culprit you were trying to catch?"

"Yes, appa, now chill. It's all fine," she said, trying to calm them down. She looked at Muthuswamy, her face asking him who informed them.

Muthuswamy smiled and shrugged as he explained, "It is just a small injury, nothing serious," he said. "The doctor said that she will be fine in a couple of days."

"Come on now," her amma picked her up, "Let's go home, I'll give you the right food and nutrition to…"

"Amma, I have work, I have to…" Before she could explain anything to her parents, she heard some sniffles. Rithika looked at Kaali and saw him wiping the corner of his eyes. She narrowed her brow and asked her parents to wait outside, "I'll be there in 5 minutes," she said seriously, and they slowly walked out.

Constable Bablu stood at the door and locked it while the other Constable Bambi stood beside Kaali, both ready with their rifles. Muthuswamy crossed his arms and stood beside Rithika as they glared at him while she handed Kaali a paper and pen. Kaali realised that they had questions about his sudden emotional outburst and started writing, "Maayi, my mother wears the same scent as that lady who entered," he hiccupped, "She was the same, getting all worried when I got hurt." He hiccupped again, and Muthuswamy poured some water from the jug on the table into a glass. All this while, his attention on Kaali remained stern, and he handed him the glass.

Holding the glass, Kaali wrote further, "This was only until last year. After that, since… since the incident… since…" His handwriting became messy, and his fingers shivered.

"Since you assaulted a deaf girl," Rithika said loudly as she started recording on her phone.

But Kaali couldn't hear her and continued writing, "Since I committed the crime, maayi is so ashamed of me that she is not talking to me. It is like two strangers are living in the same house." He wiped his eyes and cheeks. "When I saw your mother, I felt the presence of my mother…" His lower lip trembled. "I … I just…" He covered his eyes with his fingers, and a silence spread in the room.

Rithika got up from her seat, aided by Muthuswamy holding her arms, and she walked up to Kaali. "Tell me everything in detail," she asked Kaali very firmly. She tapped her tongue and then his ears, signalling him to tell her about this incident. She then pulled a chair and sat in front of him, with one leg crossed over the other. Rithika was breathing fast due to the pain in her head, but she couldn't wait to find out the truth.

Muthuswamy gestured to the constable standing at the door, and he went out. The constable approached Rithika's parents and told them, "Ma'am is busy interrogating the culprit. She will need some time. You can wait for her here, but it will be evening by then."

"Okay, we will wait…" Rithika's mother said.

"No, I know her work is important right now and it will take time. We should leave," her father said and got up, pulling his wife's arm softly.

The constable walked back into the room and locked it from inside. Kaali, who was rubbing his eyes, felt the vibration of a door hitting, and he brought his attention back to Rithika's smell in front of him. She was glaring at him without a blink. He gulped down the saliva in his mouth and continued to write, "I have regretted every moment of my life since that incident. I have worked my ass off for the hotel to pay them back for saving me. I wanted to donate some money for girls' education in my neighbourhood, but they refused, saying that I earned it from the wrong means. I didn't have enough to donate anywhere else." He scoffed, "Look at the irony of life, even for repenting one's sins, we need money." He wiped his nose with the back of his palm,

"I kept slogging off day and night, telling myself just one thing, 'I have to repent for my sins,' but the universe had decided its own ways of making me pay for my sins." He looked up at Rithika and smiled.

Muthuswamy walked near him and tapped on his ears. Kaali nodded and wrote, "A week ago, there was a beautiful young lady customer in our hotel. She would talk to me like a little brother. Smile at me, ask me how I was, and tell me to bring her things from the shops nearby." He sighed, "After a long time, someone was showing respect to me. After a long time, someone was being nice to me," he smiled faintly, "But who knew it was only to trap me," his lower lip trembled again, "She asked me to take a parcel to an address. I was happy to do anything for her. After all, she made me feel good about myself." He wiped his cheeks, "When I reached the address, there were ladies. Many of them. All were smirking at me like they caught a big hunt. They asked me to open the parcel, which they claimed was for me only." Kaali shuddered, "It had the ear machine… of the… of her…" he sobbed, "I knew my karma had come to find me, finally. The dark fear that I had in my heart was coming to reality."

As Kaali wrote the whole incident to Rithika and read it out loud, all the officers in the room were shocked to the core. They couldn't believe how this man suffered so much pain. They looked at each other and felt bad for Kaali, who was weeping uncontrollably. Suddenly, the rage against him turned to sympathy.

"In one corner of my heart, I feel they deserve punishment but then in the other corner, I feel I deserve what I got," Kaali concluded at the end of the page.

Muthuswamy approached him and with his finger, made a cross on his chest. Kaali nodded and wrote, "I guess you mean that they did wrong to me. But what will you do with them anyway? They all looked like innocent women who were just avenging the abuse of a woman." Muthuswamy took a step near him and tapped on his forehead, nose, and cheeks. Kaali sniffed and wrote, "I think you mean to ask about their faces, their facial description." Muthuswamy softly punched his chest to tell him that he was right, and Kaali started describing the women on another sheet of paper given to him.

* * *

Bablu and Bambi took a sip of their tea at the canteen of the hospital. While they had arranged the discharge papers of Rithika and Kaali, Muthuswamy had taken Kaali to the police station in his van. Rithika went home with her parents at the request of Muthuswamy and both the constables.

"What Kaali did was wrong, indeed," Bablu said as he took a bite of the vada pav.

"I know," Bambi nodded.

"So, what the women did with him was right?" Bablu asked.

Bambi shrugged when they heard the scream of a lady, "Aargghhh!!!! Please! Someone do something!" she was weeping loudly, her sobs echoing through the walls of the hospital.

Bablu and Bambi got up and walked up to the source of the sound and found an old lady screaming and crying at a nurse, holding her by her arms and pleading, "Please save her! I beg of you!"

Bablu approached the lady and asked, "What happened, amma?" He placed his palm on her shoulder.

The lady looked at him and flinched on seeing his uniform. "No!" she took a step back.

The nurse said, "Sir," and Bablu looked at her with furrowed brows, not understanding the fear behind the old lady's reaction. The nurse explained to his confused expression, "Her daughter, she… she is…"

"A demon ate her up!" the old lady said with her teeth tightly clenched. She buried her face in her palms and started to wail louder.

"What?" Bablu furrowed his brow.

"There is a lot of blood between her legs," the nurse explained, and both the constable's eyes widened. "She is in the operating theatre. The doctors are doing their job, but I requested her to go to the police…"

"No!" the lady shouted. "No police involvement!" she said through gritted teeth.

Bablu furrowed his brow, "But dear mother, we will help you, we will find out…"

"I don't want the trouble of going to the police station every other day. I don't want my daughter to tell them what happened to her and go through the same pain again!"

"But don't you want justice?" asked Bablu, and the old lady went silent. Her eyes were thoughtful, and her tears had stopped flowing.

She wiped her cheeks and said, "Nurse, I want my daughter fit and fine. " The nurse nodded, and the lady looked at the constables from the corner of her eyes and said, "Poor people only strive for food, no rights, no justice." She walked up to the operating theatre and stood outside it, her hands joined, her lips moving rigorously, chanting a mantra.

Bablu and Bambi walked out of the hospital with narrowed brows. They felt insulted as police officers and wanted to explain to the lady how they could help her. They drove back to the police station. They really wanted to provide justice to her, but her perception of the process was way too negative. The lady was not in a position to understand anything. So, they just had to leave it there.

Back home, Rithika couldn't sit peacefully. As she waited for Muthuswamy's call, she restlessly kept stomping from one corner of her room to another. At every round, she took a sip of water and rubbed her head. Her father entered her room and looked at her with folded arms. Rithika peered at him and sighed, "I want to know what further plan of action the IG has for this case. Muthuswamy will…"

TRING

Her phone rang, and Rithika rushed to her bed to pick it up. "Hello? Muthuswamy? What did the IG say?"

"Kaali is kept in the special cell for investigation because he said he didn't want to go home like this. He couldn't face his mother in this condition."

"Hmm..." Rithika nodded. "It is better for him to stay in a safe space. He is our only eyewitness of the gang."

"Yes. I took the recording and his papers to the IG, but he was busy and said that we would meet tomorrow."

"Oh, God!" Rithika murmured as she sat on the bed, her fingers running through her hair.

"It is good in a way, we can go to the IG together tomorrow and talk to him. You can convince him better than I can," he chuckled softly and then cleared his throat.

"Okay," Rithika whispered and hung up the call.

The next morning, Rithika was up and ready at 6 am. She went for a jog, had a heavy breakfast, worshipped God in the home-placed temple, and wore her police uniform after a long time. The khaki colour was her pride, her life, her everything. As she was about to leave, her dad applied a small tikka on her forehead, a small dot between her brows, and now she was ready for the big day. Today, Rithika was going to start with her duty again but not just any duty. She had all the evidence to prove that her suspicion of a gang behind all the murders, that all the murders are connected, and that there must be a gang behind it is true.

Rithika walked into the office after nearly 10 days. All the officers stood up to salute her. Some of the female constables approached her to welcome her back. Bablu walked up to her with a small red box with a yellow paisley design on it. He opened it to reveal its contents of sweets and said, "I am so glad that one of our best officers is back on duty!" He picked up a piece of sweet and fed Rithika.

Rithika took a bite of it and said, "Thank you so much, all of you!"

"But madam was never off duty, was she?" Bablu said.

"Yes!" said the officers in unison and started to clap.

Muthuswamy had just entered the station and saw them clapping. He joined them and was fed the sweet by Bablu, who was distributing it among everyone.

Rithika looked at Muthuswamy and nodded assertively. She went to sit at her desk, and Muthuswamy joined her there. Opening the file of documents in his hands, he said, "This has all the data of sexual abusers who were not convicted and then murdered by the gang. Then we have a research paper on a list of possible targets by the gang. It also has the in-detail FIR registered by Kaali yesterday against the gang, where he narrated the whole incident to us. With this solid proof, the IG will have to call a CBI inquiry."

Rithika nodded at him as she checked all the papers. Muthuswamy stared at her while she turned the pages of the file. He could see the glow on her face—the glow of the first step of victory, the glow of finding the culprit. She looked at him, and he looked away at once. But she had caught him staring at her, and her heart skipped a beat.

Rithika cleared her throat and shifted in her seat as she closed the file and said, "We should now go and meet the IG."

"Yes, yes, of course," Muthuswamy smiled.

Rithika looked at him and said, "Um, actually..."

"Yeah?"

"I wanted to say that... uh..."

"Yeah, tell me," he gazed at her intently.

Rithika threw a beam at him and said, "I wanted to thank you..." She tucked in a strand of her baby hair behind her ear. You have been my biggest supporter during this tough time. If it wasn't for you, I don't know if I would have been able to..."

"It was all your doing, Miss Rithika. You were the one who motivated me to work hard on this case; otherwise, I was quite irresponsible to look deeper into this matter," he shrugged with a smile.

Rithika felt her cheeks glow as she got up, turned around and walked towards the IG's cabin.

Seeing their exchange of sweet words, Bablu, the constable, started singing softly, "*Udta hi phiroon inn hawaaon mai kahin.*"

As the other constables giggled, Muthuswamy grinned and sat at his desk.

Rithika knocked on the door and IG Balram called out, "Come in!" She opened the door and walked in slowly. Balram saw her and said, "Oh, welcome back, Officer Rithika." He got up to greet her and extended his hand to shake. Rithika held his palm firmly and gave a strong shake, looking straight into his eyes, as if challenging him.

Balram retrieved his arm and ushered her to the chair in front of him, "Please sit."

Rithika took a seat and placed the file from her arms on the table. She opened the file and said, "Sir, I have been working with Officer Muthuswamy on the cases from Mandi, Chennai, and Mumbai. As I had said, they are all connected. Here, I have found the evidence for the same."

"Hmmm..." Balram took the file in his hand and started going through the papers. "I heard you were working very hard even after being suspended," he bobbed his head. "Sounds quite impressive of you."

Rithika said with a straight face, "I was sure of my gut intuition, and I just collected the evidence," as she saw him turning the pages of the file. She continued, "And our biggest evidence is in the security cell. His name is Kaali. His FIR report, along with his statement written by him, is attached in there. He was attacked by the gang because he had sexually molested a deaf and dumb girl a year ago. He confidently stated that they attacked him for that particular crime because the girl whom he molested was present there. They turned him deaf and dumb, just like her."

"Hmmm…" Balram's brows furrowed as he asked, "But how can you say that this gang who attacked Kaali is the same gang who committed all the previous crimes? Isn't it possible that this was just that girl's connection?"

"Possibly," she clenched her fist because he was still doubting her investigation. Her breath was turning fast, but she inhaled deeply and said, "But we can at least start a CBI inquiry on this case and find out Kaali's attackers as they have turned his life upside down. Once we find them, I am sure that we will be able to make them spit out all their crimes."

Balram nodded and said, "Okay, I would like to meet Kaali once and talk to him."

"Sure, sir. Today, at what time?"

"Right now, in 15 minutes?"

Rithika got up and saluted him. She walked out of the cabin, and all the police officers, the constables, and Muthuswamy looked at her with hope in their eyes. Rithika had a blank expression as she walked in the middle of the station and took a good 360-degree turn to look at them. Slowly, her face turned to a smile, and there was a huge round of applause for her.

"Congratulations, madam, finally the IG is looking into this matter!" Bablu told her, and she beamed at him.

* * *

Rithika reached the special investigation cell with Muthuswamy. Kaali was handcuffed to the table, a deaf translator beside him, and the room was vacant with no other furniture. The walls screamed emptiness at Kaali, and he knew something was about to happen. He suddenly felt a vibration as if a door had been shut loudly and he kept his hand on the steel table to feel the vibrations better. As he turned his head towards the door, his heart started to pound on seeing the inspector walk in front of him. There was a calmness that spread around him, not letting him understand what more was about to happen.

IG Balram and Rithika sat in front of him and started asking about the details of the women. How did they look and talk? What was the place like? What else did he hear them discuss?

It was difficult for Kaali to understand the translator as it was his first time with one. He tried hard to remember whatever he could to help the officers. Everything was so new and yet so important. The trauma of the incident had suppressed a lot of his memories. He couldn't remember much even though he tried his best. But he started weeping with helplessness.

"It's okay. Try as much as you can remember," said the psychologist sitting with him. She turned to Rithika and explained, "Too much pressure and force will affect him mentally. He may need some rest."

"No!" Rithika was furious. "He needs to give us the details; he needs to remember it all; it is important for this case!" She moved in front of Kaali, sat down on the chair in front of him, and looked deeply into his eyes. "I need you to do this," she kept her palm on his shoulder, and he held her hand to understand what she said. "You have to do this, help us catch the gang!"

Kaali nodded reassuringly and took a deep breath. After a few seconds of silence, he started to speak in his broken language that was understood by the deaf translator, and she translated it for the officers, "There were around 22 women. It seemed like it was a big gang of only women. They were there to fight against all the evils who trouble women. They all looked furious," he clenched his fists, "It seemed like they wanted to kill all the men who look down upon girls and think that they can use them as an object. At that moment, when they were about to change my life for the worse, I could feel like an object myself that they wanted to destroy just the way…" he shuddered, "The way I did."

After hearing the full story and going through three hours of investigation, Balram informed Rithika, "I will make sure that a CBI inquiry is set up."

Hearing this, finally, after so many days, Rithika beamed brightly, and her eyes turned teary. She thanked the IG and shook hands with him. As she walked out of the special investigation cell, she saw Muthuswamy walk towards her. Rithika's heart started beating faster. Her smile reached her eyes, making her cheeks glow red. She reminisced about the night when he came to pick her up from the bar when she was drunk to the brim. How he brought her home so that she didn't have to be embarrassed in front of her parents. Her chest fluttered at how he helped her work on the case, find the criminal records, search the abusers, talk to other state officers, and set his team up for the case, all without the greed of getting his name in the project.

Muthuswamy's eyes were twinkling when he saw the victorious expression on Rithika's face. He could see how happy and at peace she was. Even though they were halfway there, and the battle was yet to be won, this big step was a huge relief to them. But he knew he was there with her, supporting her, and would always stand by her side, no matter what.

Rithika took the last few steps to climb down the building and ran up to him. Without giving it much thought, his arms rose in the air as she approached him with a jump in her walk and wrapped her arms around his waist, hugging him tight. "Thank you for everything," she whispered in his ear.

"I'm always here," he whispered back as he held her shoulders tightly between his arms.

Chapter 9

New Phase Of Past Life

Rithika looked around at the silent café. It was 4:30 pm on a Sunday and only two tables were taken other than hers. The abstract paintings were hung low on the wall, making her question the emotions she felt at that moment. As she looked at the person sitting in front of her, the distinguished gentleman who had always made her feel respected and valued, just like her father, Rithika's eyes turned misty. She looked down at her white sleeveless top, the one her mother had gifted her two years back on her birthday, but she never wore it.

"Only God knows when she will finally wear this pretty dress on a date!" her mother complained a few months ago yet again when she saw that top on her cupboard shelf.

Rithika giggled internally, reminiscing about this moment and looked at the man in front of her. They had just ordered two cups of hot coffee, and Muthuswamy hung up the call he had received from his constable. He chuckled and said, "This Bambi, he just cannot keep his mouth shut. Now Bablu was calling me to give me dating tips." Rithika's cheeks turned red as he kept his phone on the table, upside down, and added, "And if it makes you feel better, the IG is at the Supreme Court to finalise a CBI inquiry."

Rithika smiled widely, and Muthuswamy looked down at the table. Her hand was placed on it, and he wanted to hold it firmly. As he slowly moved his fingers towards hers, Rithika chuckled internally and said, "We used to fight like cats and dogs."

Muthuswamy smiled at her, "Well, that was my only way to have an informal conversation with you." He peered into her eyes.

Rithika's eyes widened as she said softly, "What do you mean by that?"

With his brows confidently raised, he said, "Exactly what you are understanding..."

Rithika's jaw dropped a little as she tried to collect some words to express herself in that moment. She stuttered and fumbled before she asked softly, "Are you trying to tell me that you have liked me for such a long time?"

He shrugged, "Well, I hope that is a good surprise," he chortled.

"Yeah... yeah," she shook her head and tucked a strand of her messy hair, tied into a bun, behind her ear and said, "I mean, of course, why not, but it is, uh... a bit of a..." she scoffed.

"Shocking?" he asked her.

Her brows furrowed for a moment, "Well, I guess yes, because we always had banter and I thought that we disliked each other a lot," she giggled awkwardly.

Muthuswamy leaned in a bit closer to her and said, "Remember the first time we met, you were shouting at a constable for not filing an FIR for an old lady because she was a beggar?"

Rithika rolled her eyes, trying to remember the day, and nodded her head, "Um, yeah, I think so…"

"That was the moment I was truly fascinated by Inspector Rithika Murthy," he slowly moved his hand over the table and kept it on her fingers. "Responsible, empathetic, and a badass! I saw your best qualities at once!" he whispered in her face, and she could smell his fragrance across the table.

A rush of blush made her cheeks red, and Rithika's heart was beating fast yet calm. The waiter came to serve their coffee, and he took his hand away, clearing his throat and making her giggle again.

As they sipped their coffees together, looking at each other, Rithika again tucked a strand of her hair behind her ear, blushing at the way he stared at her. The moment was sending butterflies in her belly when her phone started to vibrate. She checked to see who was calling her, and it was her father.

"Hello, yes, appa…" she said. Yes, we are going to get permission to set up a CBI inquiry!" She chuckled as her father loudly congratulated her from the other side of the phone. Thank you so much in advance, appa!" she smiled widely.

Muthuswamy kept looking at her smile. He sighed. How much he loved her smile. Her eyes. And then it hit him. *I am in…*

"Let's go?" Rithika broke his chain of thoughts. "I am taking Amma and Appa for dinner tonight. It's been so long since I have spent time with them since I came back from Darjeeling in the midst of our vacation."

Muthuswamy nodded, "Yes, we should leave," he called the waiter and asked for the bill.

✳ ✳ ✳

The next morning, Rithika drove her van to the special investigation cell with her constables Bablu and Bambi. It was a small bungalow with chipped blue walls and a dry lawn on the outskirts of Chennai. There were no other bungalows within at least a kilometre radius, and it was a perfect spot to keep the non-convicted sexual abusers in one place.

"So, what's the update, madam?" Bablu asked Rithika as he stood behind her. "How long will we have to keep them here?" he looked around at the abusers with furrowed brows.

"At least until the time we do not get closer to the gang," she said, staring at each and every abuser.

A guy in his late 50s had a big beard and was wearing an orchid kurta. He looked fresh and clean but grumpy at the need to live here at the bungalow on the outskirts of the city of Chennai. Another man in his late 60s needed a stick to walk around as he sat at the dining table to have his breakfast. Rithika's eyes narrowed at the food that she saw, and she walked up to the table. She found well-packaged high-class food as if it had arrived from a hotel nearby and asked, "Who ordered this food?"

The man in the orchid kurta said in his deep, heavy voice, "I ordered it. I didn't want to have that bland food made in this small kitchen every day."

"And who gave you the permission to order it?" Rithika took a step towards him with her shoulders broadened.

He got up from the sofa, his height taller than hers. He was breathing down at her but before he could reply, Rithika received a call from Muthuswamy, "Hello, yes, tell me?" the man in the kurta kept staring at her with vex in his eyes. She ignored his looks and said, "Okay, bring Kaali to the centre, I am here with Bablu and Bambi." She hung up and looked back at the tall man and said, "Sir, even though you are here to keep you safe, you are here because of a crime that you committed long back," she said firmly and his eyes darted down, taking a step back, "And it doesn't matter how long it has been to that crime, you can still be convicted as we have a full report on your activities by reopening your case anytime."

The man moved a step back, and she looked around at the house. It was a small bungalow with basic amenities. Most of the criminals looked rich by their clothing and their skin shining. They had a look of attitude in their eyes but not a pinch of shame for what they had done. As she climbed up the stairs, Rithika's gut was boiling at how they felt safe and secure at the government's cost when actually they should have been in jail. How they felt that they deserved this special treatment because a murderer could kill them, but they should have been left to be killed.

Her steps stopped on the first floor as she bent down over the railing, looking down at the men sitting there. For a second, her eyes searched for a familiar face, but then she realised that she had never complained about that person.

A beautiful face with big sharp eyes flashed in front of her. Rithika's heart started beating fast when his perfectly placed straight teeth shone behind his smile, his well-shaved cheeks smelling of the aftershave. Rithika started taking deep breaths and clenched the railing tighter.

The doorbell rang, and Rithika saw Bablu open the gate. As soon as she saw Muthuswamy enter the house, her chest felt light, and she ran down the stairs. But then she realised the people around her and stopped her legs from running. Keeping her poise, she walked down slowly up to him and shook hands with Muthuswamy firmly and professionally.

"Good morning, Rithika," he said, looking deep into her eyes with a short smile, "Kaali will also stay here as the gang can try to catch him again."

Rithika nodded and looked at Kaali entering from behind, handcuffed by Bambi. Her eyes followed Kaali, but her mind was clearly somewhere else. Her eyeballs moved to the floor and back at Kaali, wandering around the living room. Muthuswamy could see that something was up with her and that her focus was not fully on the case, that she wasn't present at the moment as she always was.

"The CBI inquiry has started," Muthuswamy said as he walked towards the balcony in the other direction, ushering her to join him. "Until they find the gang, we will have to keep an eye on these people and make sure to catch the gang of murderers if they reach here," he kept looking at her, but Rithika was still lost in her thoughts. Slowly, he placed his hand on her shoulder, and she flinched. "Hey, is everything alright?"

Rithika looked at him and nodded. They stood at the balcony railing, and she paused for a second, looking out at the dried grasses. She said, "What about the tech team? Did they find any traces of the murderers online?"

Muthuswamy was still thinking about Rithika and doubting if she was really fine. But then he brought his thoughts back to their conversation and said, "Yeah, um... yes, they are searching on every social media and tracing the numbers." He cleared his throat.

Rithika's phone rang, and she picked it up immediately, "Hello? Yes, sir..."

After a few minutes, as she put the cell phone back in her pocket, she turned to Muthuswamy and said, "The tech team has found some evidence. We will have to go to the office to check it out as they aren't 100 per cent sure of what they have found."

"Let's go immediately," Muthuswamy says, placing his hand on her shoulder. She pauses, looking at his palm, which touches and moves away slightly.

Muthuswamy felt a bit ashamed of touching her. He did not want to make her uncomfortable or make her think of him as unprofessional. He quickly moved a step away and said, "I am sorry." He tried to think of more words to apologise but couldn't. His jaws hung in the air with awkwardness.

And then, breaking the silence, Rithika said, "Let's go. It is very important to catch the gang." In her last words, she rushed out of the balcony and towards the gate, followed by Muthuswamy.

Rithika drove the van hastily. She didn't even look at Muthuswamy or talk to him once. She didn't leave space for a conversation to start. She kept on honking and driving with speed, shouting at the passersby for not using the footpath to walk or the zebra crossing to cross. She kept complaining about how no one followed the rules but only wanted to do what they felt like doing.

Muthuswamy kept peering at her every now and then. He didn't stare at her directly for fear of offending her again. But he wanted to know what went wrong, why she was acting weird towards him now. He wanted to understand if he had made a mistake that was causing her not to look at him.

Is she confused about us, or is she having doubts about our relationship...

"Come on!" she pressed the brakes with force as they stopped in front of their office. Rithika collected her phone and wallet from the dashboard and stepped out of the van without looking at him. Muthuswamy's chest felt more than uneasy now as he followed her to the office.

"What's the update?" she asked the tech leader, Tanya.

Tanya, a short, heightened, plump girl with long hair and dusky skin colour, was sitting in the conference room, ready with her laptop and presentation on the big screen. "Oh, great. You arrived earlier than I expected," she said as she started her presentation. "Please have a seat. I'll start in just a minute," she said as she pressed some buttons on the keyboard.

"Okay, so," Tanya cleared her throat, "We were searching YouTube and other social media for pages and channels of this gang to find out where they communicate and keep in touch. They obviously don't have a WhatsApp or Telegram group because that is way too easy for us to track and catch them up. And as per their record of killing so many people in such a style that we couldn't get to them or even doubt that there could be a gang behind it all, they are indeed good planners. They have a tech team behind them too, for sure." Tanya pressed a button, and the YouTube video started, "This is the news of the girl from Mandi whose house was put on fire by her parents," she scrolled down to the comments and read them aloud, "Catch the perpetrators! Kill them! Kill them the same way!" she opened the reply section of that comment, "Someone needs to take action! The police are of no use!" she opened more replies and read, "Luring them back to the city! And the next comment is tying them up to the house, giving the Chinese water torture, and soon putting them on fire! Great work girls! They need to be shown just what they did! That's KARMA! That's justice in its right form!"

Rithika's eyes were glued to the screen as she read the comments that were actually a message from those women to each other. Her eyes widened at the realisation of how they communicated.

"So, we searched for more such news videos and checked their comments too," Tanya then opened another video. "The news of the little girl being raped for a month by the aged man," she sighed. "On the hills, capture him and torture him just the same way," Tanya read the date of the comment. "This comment was in the month when that man was already captured and tortured, which means…"

"That they talked in the present tense, not past," Rithika stated.

Tanya nodded when Muthuswamy said, "But this could also be just the outrage by common people, how can you be sure that these are the same women?"

"That's why we checked the profiles of all these women," Tanya replied. "We found their email IDs and hacked into them," she opened her presentation. "This is a list of most of the women in their team," she started reading out loud. "Ambika Mahajan, she was raped by her boyfriend. Tulsi Khurana was molested at a public gathering," Tanya kept on reading each name written under their photos and their history of sexual abuse. "These 14 women are the main managers of this team who had started this gang. They are also excelling in their fields such as accounts, IT, and medicine. They are still working jobs at their companies and hospitals while they work towards taking revenge on the weekends." Tanya stopped the presentation and turned towards Rithika. "They keep on recruiting people who are sexually abused or raped and are not given justice by the legal system of the country. Sadly, in many of their cases, the culprit is from a place of power, and hence, these women are enraged by injustice."

When Tanya completed her presentation, IG Balram walked into the conference room. Rithika and Muthuswamy got up from their seats and saluted him. Balram gestured for them to sit down and took a deep breath before speaking up, "I heard you found the names and identities of most of the gang members?" he looked at Tanya.

She nodded at him, "Yes, sir."

"I am sorry I couldn't be at this meeting because," he looked at Rithika, sighed, and continued, "Rithika, we have news," his face turned serious, "A small district in West Bengal is in a rage due to the girls being sexually abused by..." his jaw hung low, "by a political leader there..." Rithika got up from her seat, "I know, Rithika, it is a very serious and difficult matter. But I know only you can solve it. I know only you can go against a political leader without fear."

"Send me the details of the inspector in charge of that district. I'll take a flight there right away," Rithika said through clenched teeth.

"Don't worry about the inspector, there is a chance of this gang..." he looked at the screen, "...this gang of women murdering those sexual abusers by approaching the political leader. So, a couple of officers from the CBI team will accompany you." Balram looked at Muthuswamy and said, "And you will aid the CBI team here in Chennai. They are planning to visit other cities like Mumbai and Darjeeling soon." Balram sighed deeply, got up from his seat, and looked at Rithika, "I hope looking at your passion towards this case, I am sure the gang will be caught very soon."

Rithika was about to leave, but hearing Balram's last words, she stopped and said, "Why just the gang, sir?" she peered into his eyes, "Why are we more inclined towards catching the gang and not the political leader who abused his power? Why do we want to put in all our energy to catch the gang trying to provide justice, though in a wrong manner, but…" she looked down at the table, "I am sorry, sir, but… I think somewhere it is the mistake of the system that a gang started working against us or, in a way, in favour of the common people, trying to provide justice. Don't you think?" she looked at Tanya, and she started with the presentation, "Just look at the faces of these girls; where do they look like criminals? Their eyes are still crying for justice because even if they killed an abuser, even if they avenged them, they are still hurt that their own country's system couldn't provide them with justice. When they tried to fight for it, they became criminals themselves in the eyes of the system, which should have helped them and healed them. Maybe we could have stopped this gang from forming in the first place?"

"In the end, they chose the wrong path, Rithika, so how are we to be blamed for it?"

"Didn't we, didn't our system choose the wrong path by bowing in front of the leaders and not providing these innocents their justice?" Rithika's eyes turned misty. "Didn't a wrong system turn them towards the wrong path?" A drop of tear fell down her cheek, and Muthuswamy kept staring at her vulnerable state. There was silence in the room, and no one said anything for the next minute. Muthuswamy was finding it difficult to understand how Rithika, the strong woman he had always known, became so emotional about a particular case. He couldn't understand why she was getting attached to the case as if it were her own.

His heart started beating fast as he realised that he doubted the answer to this question he had just had.

Chapter 10

Leader Lures Ladies

Rithika hugged her parents, picked up her bag, and stepped out of the house. Her feet crossed the boundary but stopped mid-air. She contemplated talking to her father about why she decided to become a police officer. Her eyes turned to the corner as she kept her feet on the threshold. Taking a deep breath, she took another step and left the house.

Taking a flight and then a car to the village of Sandhya in West Bengal, Rithika remained quiet all the way while her colleagues, Aman and Jeet, the CBI officers, discussed their lives and work. They got down to the village police station and met the station inspector.

After the initial greetings, they sat down at the table and Rithika was the first one to start, "What is the update on catching that political leader?" she peered straight into the eyes of the inspector.

Inspector Roy scoffed and said, "But you have just arrived, what do you expect me to..."

"I don't need to expect anything from you," Rithika said. "Hundreds already expect you of villagers." She opened a file in her hand. "As per the reports and news channels, you have been receiving complaints from women of different age groups for more than a year now." She glared into his eyes. "And Mr. Roy, I believe the whole village is under you." She turned the page of the file. "And yet, to date, you have received 189 complaints from women and their husbands, brothers, fathers…"

"This is not the correct report, I'll give you…" Roy tried to clarify.

"I have received this report from the centre where your police station and every police station in the country update the cases filed from their district," Rithika raised her voice, and Roy went silent. He kept looking at her as she continued, "So, out of a total of 559 families here, you received a total of 189 complaints. This comprises mostly of women. Which," she picked up the calculator, "As per my calculation is more than half of the women in your village, under YOUR guidance have gone through sexual assault and you did NOTHING!" she kept glaring into his eyes.

Roy shook his head. "This is not done. You are a guest here, and I was doing my duty to make you feel at home, but you are only trying to insult me and my work…" He got up from his seat.

Rithika chuckled, giggled, and slowly started laughing as she got up and patted Roy on his shoulder, "Do you think that I am your sister or relative? Or your friend? Or your in-law?" Her laughter faded as she screamed at the top of her lungs, "Then WHY do I need to feel at HOME?"

Hearing her shout, Aman and Jeet got up from their seats. Roy looked to his left and right, feeling humiliated in front of his havildars. He tried to say something, but Rithika cut him off, "This is not my home. A place where so many women are assaulted and on top of that not heard, their grievances are not heard, this CANNOT be my home," Her eyes turned wide like Goddess Kali as her breath was rapid and unsteady, her forehead sweating.

"Inspector Rithika," Aman called out to her, "I think we should settle down and start the work tomorrow morning. It is already late evening."

Jeet stuttered as he was already taken aback by Rithika's behaviour, "Yes, ma'am, I think it is too late to discuss this now, we came here just to meet the officer in charge. Let's solve it tomorrow."

Rithika took a step back, her gaze not faltering from Roy, and said, "We will discuss directly with the women of the village tomorrow," she turned around. "Call a *panchayat!*" she announced. "Tomorrow morning at 7 am, sharp."

Rithika walked out of the station, followed by Aman and Jeet. Two havildars saluted her, while a lady constable, with misty eyes, saw the woman power on duty in her office.

That night, Rithika couldn't sleep. She kept turning and tumbling on her bed. There was silence in her room, and the crickets chirping outside were adding to the peace. However, the exterior did not positively affect her because her inside was going through a war. Rithika picked up her phone and saw another missed call from Muthuswamy. She had received 7 missed calls that day. But she didn't feel like talking to him.

He is not at fault. She told herself as her eyes turned misty and her throat tightened. *But he needs to know the truth. I cannot run away from it if I want to be with him. He has all the right to know about it.* She wiped her eyes and blew her nose on a tissue paper.

Rithika got up from her bed, held her phone, and opened her call history. As her thumb hovered above Muthuswamy's name, she took a deep breath and was about to click on it when she heard a knock on the door.

Her thumb stopped mid-air, and she threw the phone on the bed. Getting up, she heard another knock on the door and called out, "Coming!"

Rithika straightened her nightshirt and brought her hair forward. Clearing her throat, she opened the door and saw a tall, well-built man standing in front of her, surrounded by healthy women.

"Yes?" she asked them, her brows furrowed. "Who are you?"

"Inspector, Miss Rithika?" said the man.

"Yaa, tell me?" she looked at the women standing there with folded hands.

"Can we come inside to talk to you?"

Rithika thought briefly and said, "Why don't we have this meeting downstairs in the lounge?"

The woman smirked as the man said, "You are forgetting this is a village. And this is a Dharamshala."

"Yes, I meant just downstairs instead of my room."

The women looked at each other and hurried inside the room, pushing Rithika by her shoulder as she said loudly, "Hey! What's happening? You cannot enter my room without my permission…"

The man entered last while a lady stood at the door wide open. Keeping his fists on his waist, the man said, "Chill, we are not going to harm you. We are here to talk to you, in private." He forced a smile on his face and Rithika knew something was up.

Rithika moved back, taking a few steps towards the door, and held a water jug tightly in her hands. Observing her movement, the man said, "It is okay, you can hold anything for safety. But remember, these women are here for your safety."

Rithika furrowed her brows and said, "Who ARE you and WHY are you here?"

The man said, "Finally, we are back on the topic." He sighed, "Okay, so my name is Zafar, and I am the little brother of Sarfaraaz," he paused before continuing, "I am here only to tell you that the women who are blaming my big brother for assaulting them sexually are actually lying." Rithika rolled her eyes as he said, "No, hear me out. I am telling you the truth. Let me show you the proof," he brought out his phone and showed her the pictures of Sarfaraaz with various women of the village, smiling and chatting. Rithika took the phone in her hand and looked at the pictures carefully. They indeed looked happy and close.

Zafar said, "Tomorrow morning in the panchayat those women will talk all nonsense to you about my brother and me. I am sure you already believe them, but I just wanted to tell you our side of the story. These women tried to seduce my brother by showing their cleavage every time he passed them, dropped their dupattas, and smiled at him. They thought that they could lure him in and get his money, but when they didn't get anything more than physical affection, they filed a case of assault."

Rithika's eyes narrowed as she glared at him and he continued, "I have sent these pictures to your phone so that you can have a clear look at them and think about where your loyalties lie," he smirked at her, took a step closer as Rithika's foot moved behind, and he said softly, "It is better that you stay loyal to us, after all, we are the leaders and if you find it difficult to help us, then only GOD can help you." He smiled widely, showing his gold teeth shining brightly.

As Zafar and his women walked out of the room, Rithika's heartbeat quickened. Memories flashed in front of her eyes, and she slumped onto the bed.

Uncles are everything after one's father, my child. Stay loyal, do not speak a word, otherwise...

The hoarse voice echoed in her brain like a black liquid pouring into her mind and heart. Her chest wasn't able to breathe fully anymore, and she started inhaling deeply. Rithika's voice stuck in her throat as she tried to breathe, but she started sobbing and weeping as the memories flashed, more voices.

Why would you wear those miniskirts when I would visit? Or those blouse-like tops? Huh?

His rough palms would brush against her cheeks.

Don't blame me if you want me. Otherwise...

Otherwise, your father will hate you!

TRING!

In the silence of the night, her phone rang again, and Rithika jumped in her seat. Muthuswamy was calling her for the 10th time that day. She kept staring at his call flashing on her screen but couldn't bring herself to pick it up.

Tears rolled down her cheeks as she stood in the same position as if she were frozen. Her body denied moving, and her thumb hovered over his name.

Muthu, I want to tell you, but... I am scared...

She whispered her thoughts and fell flat on the bed, her tears still rolling down with her eyes shut tight.

* * *

The next morning, Rithika woke up early at 5 am. She felt fresh, and her mind was clearer than the previous night. "Exhaustion makes you emotional!" she murmured as she slipped on her uniform and got ready for the *panchayat.*

It was 6 am. Rithika locked her room and walked out of the Dharamshala. The chilled climate made her blow air into her palms and rub them against each other. She could see some women sweeping the floor while some were already there working on the farms. Some were taking their kids to school while some were cooking in the kitchen. Rithika couldn't find any men out and about in the village early in the morning like the women. She searched and tried to understand the situation, but she couldn't.

She reached the police station, met Aman and Jeet, and discussed the reports. Then, they met the panchayat head and discussed the same. In between her meetings, she saw the women who had entered her room late at night. Her brows narrowed when she saw them. *What are they doing here? Are they keeping an eye on me? Should I tell the CBI officers, Aman and Jeet, about this?*

Rithika opened the pictures sent to her by Zafar last night and got up from her seat to go to a corner under a tree. She looked at each of them carefully. The women of the village were smiling in the pictures as Sarfaraaz held them by their shoulders and waist on both his sides. He smiled widely, but there was a hint of uneasiness on the faces of the women. Their body language was detached from him as if they didn't want to be held by him. She looked more carefully and could see his fingers digging into the skin of their waists, as if trying to clench onto them, with the fear of them running away. Rithika's breath started turning rapid. She took shallow breaths very quickly, her chest pounding and her brows wrinkled. All the bodyguard women in black kept staring at her, and Rithika took her seat back beside the CBI officers.

Aman saw the tension on her face and asked, "Are you alright?" Rithika was deep in her thoughts, and he repeated, "Rithika? What's wrong?"

"Huh?" She shook her head and said, "No, nothing; I am fine."

"So," Jeet continued, "As I was saying, most of the women have complained that Sarfaraaz holds them inappropriately without their consent." Hearing this, Rithika was all ears to Jeet as he continued, "They say in their report that they felt uncomfortable and asked him to leave but he didn't listen to them and kept on pressing their bodies against his."

Rithika clenched her mobile phone tightly. Her blood was boiling as she glared at the women in black bodyguards roaming around her, trying to understand the whole situation.

The panchayat was set to start sharp at 7 am, and all the villagers arrived on time. While Rithika settled with Jeet and Aman along with the panchayat head, she saw Sarfaraaz settle with his women bodyguards on the opposite side. Rithika looked at the crowd of women sitting in front of her and found some familiar faces from the pictures on her phone. She looked at them, stood in front of the villagers, and said on the mic, "Today we are here to provide justice which is possible only if you are able to tell me the whole truth, clear and loud," she looked at the women nodding, and asked one of the familiar faces to narrate her story, "Do not feel shy or ashamed. You have done nothing wrong. Just tell us the truth, the way it happened."

The woman, who wore a cream saree, got up from her seat and said, "Madam, he said," she pointed at Sarafaraaz, "He said that…" his breathing turned rapid, "That he will teach us how to earn more money in our farms. He said that he will give us training and…" her brows narrowed as she spoke softly, "And how to also make our husbands work." There were hushes all around as she continued, "We all thought that being a leader, he would help us with training but when we went there, we were shocked. He tried to come close while talking to us. He wrapped his hand around our waists and pulled us close. He said that…" she took a deep breath, "That this is the only way our husbands will feel jealous and do everything for us." The lady started crying, "I did not like it at all. I pushed him away but he…"

"Did he take pictures of you?" Rithika asked, and Sarfaraaz pursed his eyes.

The lady nodded, "Yes, madam. Right when we reached there, he asked us to smile into the camera and click our pictures. But while taking the pictures, he suddenly held us tight and…"

For an hour, every lady described what they went through. Some of them cried while others spat at Sarfaraaz. Their husbands and brothers felt ashamed for not being able to protect their women. The panchayat head looked horrified by the details described by the women.

In the end, it was Sarfaraaz's chance to speak up. He got up from his seat, caressed his beard, and cleared his throat. "I don't have much to say. I have already sent the proof to Miss Rithika. She has seen our pictures together," he said, spreading his arms towards the women. They look happy and…"

"They looked uncomfortable," Rithika snapped. "They looked annoyed and wanted to kick you. They didn't like your touch, and that's what the pictures say. CLEARLY. You were holding them forcefully, and as the women said, it was at the start itself that you clicked those pictures when they didn't know what was about to happen. So, you tricked them into smiling, but you couldn't trick them into looking comfortable. You couldn't trick them into looking warm, enjoyable, or agreeable with whatever you were doing. However, you were touching them in the name of taking a picture so that you could use it in the future against them," she said in a breath and inhaled deeply at the end of her statement. Rithika then walked up to the panchayat heads' team and showed them the pictures.

The head of the panchayat got up from his seat and said, "The panchayat will give its verdict in an hour."

Rithika entered the meeting room where Aman and Jeet were waiting for her.

"I still don't get it, Rithika," Aman said. "What is up with all this *panchayat* scene? Why did we need it?"

"Exactly, we are a team of CBI officials," Jeet got up from his seat. "What will the village think about us? That even CBI officers need the help of a panchayat?"

"You guys are taking it all wrong. The panchayat was just a drama," Rithika threw her hand in the air. Aman and Jeet looked at each other, and she continued to explain their confused faces, "Look, I knew that the culprit Sarfaraaz and his people would try to lure us in by showing that they are the innocent ones," she sighed, "I knew that they would try to pull us on their side by giving in something." She stared at them, and shrugged, "And my plan worked," she brought out her phone with a smile, "Look at these pictures," she handed the phone to them.

Aman and Jeet took a careful look at the pictures of Sarfaraaz holding the women. The women had an uncomfortable smile on their faces while his fingers were digging into their waists.

"What are you trying to tell us?" Jeet asked.

"See, when the culprit found out that we were going to hold a panchayat for this case, he became very careless thinking that we officers were not that courageous or expert enough. They thought that showing us these photos would make us think that they were actually innocent, and these ladies came to them on their own and thus it will bring us on their sides." She scoffed, "And my plan worked. He showed me these photos and I could clearly see the emotions behind these photos." Aman and Jeet nodded at her as she continued, "Another reason to hold a panchayat was also that these women felt more comfortable here, as compared to a court, to share their horrific experiences."

"So, what's the next plan?" Aman asked. "How do you plan to prove him guilty and drag him to court?"

"We will take his forensic reports as well as those of the women he raped, his CCTV footage from near his areas, and finally, his phone data which our cyber team will hack," Rithika folded her hands, "And then, taking all the data on this abuser, we will reach the High Court in Kolkata!"

* * *

An hour later, the panchayat was resumed to give its verdict wherein Rithika approached the head and whispered something into his ear. The head nodded and gave the mic to Rithika who then took the dais to announce, "The women who accused Sarfaraaz of rape are sent to the city of Kolkata for a check-up. The police officers of this village along with the CBI team have retrieved the CCTV reports from his area," she took a deep breath, "My dear villagers, we have enough evidence and witnesses to take Sarafaraz to the court for a case."

Sarfaraaz's eyes widened as the abused women sitting in front of her screamed in relief, joining their hands to thank Rithika and weeping with happiness.

Rithika looked at Sarfaraaz and said, "If the state government, which is responsible for protection, creates such a situation where the protector becomes the aggressor, violator, and infringer of their basic human rights, there is no place for such leaders, and the entire system is responsible for it."

"This is not right, madam officer," Sarfaraaz got up from his seat as he was held by Aman and Jeet and handcuffed in front of everyone. "You will pay for this! My people won't leave you!" he screamed.

With pride filling up her chest, she saw Sarfaraaz being dragged to police custody when all the women pounced on her to hug her, thank her, and kiss the back of her palms.

Chapter 11

Don't Tell Anyone

Rithika reached Dharamshala to pack her bags when she saw the face her heart was yearning for. Her breathing turned rapid as she saw Muthuswamy's strong and muscular body appear in front of her. Her face started breaking down as she marched up to him. On their own, Muthuswamy's arms spread out, and she jumped into his arms, hugging him, caressing her face on his shoulder, and feeling at peace.

"Thank you so much for coming. I really needed you," she whispered.

"I know, I knew something was up," he said, "But I also knew that you wouldn't call me up or try to take my help," he caressed her hair.

Rithika took a deep breath as she retreated and wiped her cheeks, "I am fine, thank you."

Muthuswamy kept looking at her, and after a long pause, he said, "Let's have some Macher Malai Curry," he smiled.

She nodded, "Yes, they serve there at my Dharamshala."

"Amazing! Let's go then!" he ushered her, and they took a walk.

After catching up with the progress of their cases, they had their lunch. Muthuswamy then booked a room and kept his bags there. They took a walk in the garden behind the Dharamshala as he geared up to ask her the question.

"So," Muthu cleared his throat, "The progress is quite impressive. I am sure you are going to catch the gang very soon," he said.

Rithika nodded, "I… we have to. It is very important. This case is really… very important…" she whispered the last words.

"Rithika," he stopped and turned to her, "I have seen your work on so many cases. You have been very passionate about your work, and I truly admire that. But…" he took a breath, "but the way you are so involved in this case, the way you are kind of…" he sought for words, "You are emotionally involved, Rithika. That's what I have observed. Please don't be offended. It is just that you are different in this case, are you getting me? What I am trying to say is…"

"I know," she nodded and looked away, "I very well understand what you are trying to say…" Her breath trembled as she rubbed her palms on her arms, "Muthuswamy," her jaws hung as she looked at him, "I have been meaning to tell you something."

"Yes, Rithika, I am all ears," he narrowed his brow and was ready to listen to her keenly.

"I… when I was…" she took a deep breath and trembled again, "I was, I don't know how it happened but…" her lower lip quivered, "I tried to stop it, but I was a little innocent girl and," she started weeping, covering her face with her palm. She turned around.

Muthuswamy held her by the shoulders and shushed her, "Please calm down and tell me what happened."

Rithika took deep breaths and wiped her cheeks. Muthuswamy made her sit on a bench nearby. He sat silently beside her, looking at her, giving her the time to speak.

"He was papa's step-brother. After my grandmother's death, my grandfather married again when papa was 15. But they had a good relationship. No bitterness between the brothers. That's what I had been told, always." She shuddered, "It started when I was 8 years old. I was a plump kid. He would bring me chocolates, and toffees and kiss my cheeks. He would always ask me if I liked lollipops or candies, and I said lollipops. He would then ask me my favourite flavour and giggle. He would take me home, telling my parents that he was taking me to watch movies in his new home theatre. We would watch cartoons. All the time, he would stick to me, hold me tight, and keep kissing me. And by the end of the cartoon movies, he would say that he had the special lollipops. And then..." she started sobbing, "he would...he would hold my-y-y...my head so tight, tie my hair into a ponytail, and pull my hair so hard, telling me to suc-k the lolli..." she broke down, wailing into her palms, and her body kept shivering.

Muthuswamy contemplated whether to touch her shoulders to console her or not. His heart was crying for her and really wanted to comfort her. He couldn't understand what exactly to say at that moment, and he just sat there quietly, being there for her silently.

* * *

That afternoon at the police station, CBI officer Aman informed Rithika, "Sarfaraaz will be taken to Kolkata court tomorrow morning. " She beamed widely. "You are a great officer, Miss Rithika. " He put forth his hand to shake her, and she shook with pride.

"But we will have to go with him," Jeet also shook hands with her, "Congratulations!" he beamed. "So, as I was saying, we will have to go with him because there is a huge chance that the gang will come behind us on our way."

Rithika nodded, "I will be there in his van, handcuffing him with me." She looked at Muthuswamy, and he nodded with pride.

"I will be there with the driver in your van," Aman said.

"I will keep an eye from the van behind," Jeet added.

* * *

Rithika glared at Sarfaraaz as she sat beside him in the van. Their hands were tied together with handcuffs, and Aman settled in the front of the van. "Ready?" he asked her. As the other two constables settled in the van with Rithika and Sarfaraaz, she gave him a thumbs-up to leave.

The van sped through the highway, another police van right behind it. Both of them had their sirens on as other vehicles made way for them to pass. They passed through a lake connected to a river, and soon, the van was on the bridge. As the cold breeze of the morning passed through the windows, the van suddenly came to a halt. Rithika's brows narrowed as she looked ahead and asked Aman, "What's the matter?"

Aman opened the window between her and the passenger seat and said, "A big fat old man is lying on the ground. I'll go and check. " He then opened the door of his van when Jeet appeared at his window.

"Wait," he said, "I'll check, you don't take any risk," Jeet walked ahead and reached the man. The man was wearing a white shirt and khaki pants. He looked quite fat even from behind as Jeet tried to call out to him, "Hey! Man, wake up, I mean, get up, what's… what's wrong?" He touched him delicately with his stick as Rithika stared deeply at the scene unfolding in front of her through the small window, her palms tightly clenched to Sarfaraaz's handcuff.

The old man did not move, and there was no other option. Jeet bent down and touched the man's shoulder, trying to move his face towards him. He looked 50-plus and had a light beard. His eyes were closed, and he had no wound marks on his body. Jeet turned behind, facing the vans, and said, "We will have to call for backup for this case, a new one," he called out to Aman who got out of the van.

"Jeet!" Aman screamed as he saw the old man hold Jeet's feet. Jeet lost his balance and fell flat on his knees when his feet were taken hold of by the man.

Suddenly, the sunny morning turned pink as women wearing pink dresses, kurtis, and sarees surrounded the two vans. Rithika looked around, and Kaali's confession rang in her head when he said that the group of women who tortured him wore all pink.

Rithika leaned her head out of the van and screamed, "This is the gang!"

The old man left Jeet and ran up to the van where Rithika was sitting. He pulled out a gun and aimed it at Rithika.

Aman and Jeet looked at each other and removed their guns from their pockets. All the constables got out of both vans and surrounded the van with Sarfaraaz in it. Sarfaraaz's brows narrowed as he couldn't understand what was going on. He had expected his men to come and save him, but he couldn't understand which was this other gang that had come to rescue him.

Rithika took out the pistol from her pocket and held both of Sarfaraaz's wrists in her other hand. She looked around carefully until her gaze landed on the old man. Her gaze narrowed and her brows wrinkled as she stared at the man when she heard a woman's voice loud and clear.

"Give us Sarfaraaz!" said the woman. "And we will let you go!"

Rithika's chest started pounding, and she took a few deep breaths to calm herself. She wanted to speak to the gang head, but she couldn't talk from inside the vehicle and couldn't go out with Sarfaraaz.

Aman called out, "Get out of our way, otherwise it won't be good for you!"

"We know that you all are disappointed in our police force," Jeet explained, "But trust us, we will get this criminal the punishment he deserves. We will provide justice to the women of Sandhya village."

The lady who had previously spoken started laughing aloud. Her laughter turned to a roar as she mimicked what Jeet said: "We will provide justice to the women of Sandhya village!" She teased him and shouted, "And will that take away the pain of thousands of women of this gang of DISHA? Or will that punish the other criminals hiding in your secret house?"

Rithika heard the name of the gang for the first time. She found out for the first time what this gang's motive was: to give direction, Disha, to the victims.

"We are doing what we can!" Aman called out.

"No, you are not!" screamed the lady. "He is a politician for God's sake! You want me to believe that you will punish HIM?" She cringed at Sarfaraaz as she pointed at him and said, "Give him to us!"

"GIVE GIVE GIVE!" all the women in pink started chanting, asking for the criminal to be handed over to them as if he were a pig for slaughter.

Rithika's mind was racing as she couldn't help but think about who the old man was. But then she shifted her focus towards the lady and said, "Let us go! I assure you I will catch each and every criminal and get him arrested, punished, and hanged!"

"Even your step-uncle?" said the lady, and Rithika's eyes widened. She was realising how thorough their research was. She was realising how deeply they had information about each and every person they were facing.

But Rithika couldn't face defeat and said, "A strong independent gang of women making an old man bait for their mission, huh?"

The lady cackled, "Look carefully, this bald man whom you were searching for from the hospital…"

And it clicked, Rithika, "Ganja?" she said.

The lady laughed, "I like your memory strength, Rithika!"

Rithika's blood boiled because a criminal called her by her name. She pointed the gun sharply at the lady talking to her.

"Oh-ow!" said the lady. "Don't get so hyped up, girls," she took a step towards the van followed by other women in pink.

"Stop!" shouted Aman. "Do not take another step towards us!" he screamed at the top of his lungs. "I am warning you!" He clenched the gun tightly in his fingers as he saw the pink shade getting clearer with each step.

"Call for backup!" Jeet screamed on the phone. "Call for backup!"

"Give us Sarfaraaz!" shouted the lady again.

"Ganja!" said Rithika. "How come you are on their side? Hadn't they come to kill you?"

"I was an innocent who took the blame on myself to save my son! Isn't that a bigger sin?" he cried. "So, I took their side to wash my sins!" he remembered the moment when he screamed on his bed, *"I will join you!"* he had told the lady in pink who was trying to kill him. When she heard this, at once she put the oxygen mask back.

"But they will kill you once they have used you!" Rithika told him.

"Better than the jail and being hated by my wife!" said Ganja.

"Ganja!" called out the lady in the pink headscarf, "We want Sarfaraaz ALIVE!"

Ganja pointed at Rithika as she pointed at Sarfaraaz, and Rithika called out, "I'll kill him if you take another step towards me!"

"NO!" the lady screamed as her steps jolted towards Rithika's van, shouting, "NOW!"

All the women in pink marched towards the van, the constables surrounding the van, and the CBI officers Aman and Jeet.

"FIRE!" Aman ordered, and each of the constables shot a woman in pink, the bullet passing right through her chest.

But there were more. Far more than the people on the police's side, they held the constables and the CBI officers, banged inside the van as the head lady entered it.

Rithika was pointing the gun at Sarfaraaz, sweat trickling down her head. The lady in pink took a step inside the van and said, "Stop trying so hard! I know you want us, the pink gang of DISHA, to win!" She stepped closer to Rithika, whose gun was pointing right at her chest as she continued, "Give me Sarfaraaz and you'll be happier with your decision. I promise to make your step-uncle my next target. He is already on our hitlist!"

Rithika's grip loosened on her gun as the awful memories flashed in front of her eyes. She looked around at her colleagues being held by two women each and then she glared at Sarfaraaz.

"Don't think so much. Neither do you have the option to choose, nor does your heart want to!" the lady said, and Rithika gazed into her eyes.

Rithika's body loosened its grip from Sarfaraaz's wrist as if she was about to leave him and hand him over to the lady when Rithika's gun changed its course, and she shot him dead.

The lady's eyes widened, and her jaw dropped as she covered her face, which had splashes of Sarfaraaz's blood. The sudden and unexpected bullet fired at the criminal made the lady lose focus on the inspector, and Rithika wrapped her hand around the lady's neck, pointing her gun at her head.

"You are not always right!" Rithika said under clenched teeth.

Chapter 12

The Game Begins

"The head of the pink gang has been caught!" the news reporter announced on television.

"Culprit of hundreds of women in Sandhya village shot dead in the ceasefire, let us see what Inspector Rithika has to say about this?" the reporter ran towards the staircases of the high court with a mic in her hand and shoved it in front of Rithika's mouth, "Inspector, can you describe the ceasefire in which political leader Sarfaraaz died?"

"It was a heavy ceasefire from both ends. Our team tried to capture the head of the gang while they wanted the culprit for themselves. In this to and fro firing, a bullet killed Sarfaraaz on the spot, but we captured the dangerous and most wanted head of the gang,"

"Ma'am, you have shown a great deal of heroism to the people of our country, especially women. What message do you have for them?"

Ritika paused and looked far away into oblivion, recollecting every moment of her struggle towards the case as the faces of Muthuswamy, Bablu, and Bambi flashed in front of her eyes.

With a slight smile etched on her face, she looked at the reporter and said, "It is not my heroism." She sighed, "It is a collective effort of my team, Inspector Muthuswamy, and our constables Bambi and Bablu. Without their support, I wouldn't have been able to crack this case."

"So, do you think even men can empathise over such women's issues that include heinous crimes like rape and sexual molestation? Or do we really need a gang of women such as Disha or do we..."

"No, we don't!" Rithika said at once. "We don't need just a gang of women but a collective effort by every gender, including men and young boys who need to be included in the programme of protecting women. Unless that happens, it's difficult to achieve progress on its own."

"Right!" the reporter said, and Rithika smiled at the screen as she saw herself on the television at the police station.

IG Balram beamed at her and put his hand out. "I knew you could do this!" He shook her hand.

"Thank you, sir, it is also your support that has aided me in this case."

Balram nodded, "Rithika, our next step is to make this lady speak up." They walked to the custody room, where the pink ganghead lady was handcuffed to the table when Muthuswamy arrived with a packet. Rithika's heart skipped a beat when she saw him, as she wanted her parents to meet him as soon as possible.

Balram cleared his throat and said, "Well, now, since we are at the end of this case, I guess we can take a short break to focus on our personal lives." He beamed at the duo and patted Muthuswamy's arm. Rithika felt blood rush to her cheeks as she observed Muthuswamy look down, red-faced.

"We will, sir, but right now, we have to focus on getting the whole gang captured," he said firmly. "And we have received a parcel," he showed a neatly wrapped brown paper and said, "Let's check this…"

"I'll get to work, you guys carry on with the case and keep me updated," Balram walked out.

In the AV room, Rithika and Muthuswamy sat down at their seats as Muthuswamy inserted the CD into the drive and played it. They looked into each other's eyes when they heard a voice, "What heartfelt love you guys have."

Rithika's brow narrowed as she looked at the screen.

A lady in a grey t-shirt and a blurred face chuckled at them, "I know you two are watching this video. The idol of humanity, and the saviour of law!" she scoffed on the screen as Rithika and Muthuswamy looked at each other and then back at the screen, "You think you caught me huh? The woman who kills those who commit sexual violence against women, the woman who started with the gang to punish the ones who were able to abet their cases and run free," she clicked her tongue, "Out of lakhs of such cases that take place, only a tiny bit get reported while a tinier bit reaches the court and the tiniest of them all get convicted, but only a few go through the punishment." She paused and looked at the screen with narrowed brows, "And you think that you are the saviour of humanity and the law, both? Someone who can take care of humanity with the law?" she giggled, "Doesn't that sound funny after the facts that 1 out of a lakh case gets convicted?" she screamed on the screen, "DO YOU REALLY THINK THAT YOU ARE DOING SOMETHING RIGHT?"

The video shut down, and there were a total of 3 files named serial-wise. Rithika leaned from her chair and clicked on number 2. It opened at once, and the same woman with the grey t-shirt and blurred face spoke, "Inspector Rithika Murthy, class of 2012, these are your high school pictures, right?" She showed a picture on the screen, and Rithika's eyes widened as her brows narrowed to look at the picture carefully. The lady continued, "What happened? Are you shocked that I have this picture?" She scoffed again, "Remember Dishanath Iyer?" She showed another group picture of Rithika's high school days, "That's you, right? And this is…" On the screen, the lady in grey tapped on the lady beside Rithika in the photo, "Dishanath Iyer…" She smiled, "I am sure you remember your best friend, but do you remember what she wanted to be? When you told her about becoming a police officer, she said that she wants to become a…"

"Doctor…" Rithika whispered.

"The same doctor whose case was ongoing when you became a police officer," said the lady on the screen, "The same doctor on whose case you were not allowed to work because you were new, and you didn't even care to check who she was. And the same doctor whom you called to inform about your achievements, but you couldn't reach her call."

Rithika's heart started beating fast as she covered her mouth, and the woman continued, "And you couldn't reach her, you forgot about her…. Remember the case of the woman doctor being gang-raped in a truck? Remember her story? She was coming from a party, and hence society blamed it on her clothes and drunkard state for being raped?" the lady on the screen wiped her cheeks as she croaked, "It was MY birthday party! And she was my childhood BEST friend!" the video switched off.

Muthuswamy turned to Rithika, who was now in tears. He wrapped his arm around her shoulders as he played the next video, and the lady appeared on the screen again: "Your so-called police department rejected her parents' plea; they ignored her case to pay attention to the more profitable cases. But I kept working. Even though I am a chemical graduate, I learned MMA from Israel, followed various YouTube channels, and learned medicine from China—ALL this only since the case of Disha!"

Rithika dropped onto the chair beside, aided by Muthuswamy as the woman continued, "Hence my gang's name is Disha!" she paused, "And what do you think? You have caught me, huh? That day you caught a head of our team, and you thought you had caught Disha? The gang leader?" she scoffed, "Rithika, Disha is not a woman, it is a THOUGHT! It is not a gang, but a MOMENT! You can NEVER catch her! She can never be caught! We all are DISHA!"

Her screen gets smaller, and many other women in different-coloured T-shirts and different hairstyles appear on the screen with blurred faces, all screaming, "I AM DISHA!"

"I AM DISHA!"

"I AM DISHA!"

"I AM DISHA!"

"I AM DISHA!"

"I AM DISHA!"

The screen goes blank and there is silence in the cabin. Muthuswamy stares at Rithika, giving her the time to think, absorb, and reflect. She is staring at the screen, her eyes misty and her breath shallow. She is thinking deeply. Muthu could tell. She was in another realm. He wanted to talk to her, console her, caress her, and tell her that they would catch Disha. But did she want to catch her anymore? What Rithika wanted was the question lingering in his mind; for the first time in his life, he wasn't sure of what she wanted.

TRING

Rithika's phone rang, flashing the name "Unknown Caller."

She picked it up at once and said, "Hello?"

"I am in Amsterdam. Still alive,"

"Disha?" Rithika whispered.

"Thousands of women are trafficked from the South Asian countries to Amsterdam. Let's see how much justice I will prevail here…"

"So, you have left India?" Rithika asked softly, not understanding how to react.

"For the time being. I cannot leave India permanently, can I? Disha lived there. You, her long-lost friend, live there," she paused and then said in a coarse voice, "So, how can I leave India? It needs me the most!"

Rithika's jaw hung low as she thought of words to speak. When Muthuswamy said loudly, "What do you want from us? Why send all those videos?"

"You need to work," she said firmly, "Make separate women's police stations, have women's courts, ensure immediate disposal of cases, special procedural laws for handling these cases to ensure speedy disposal and identity protection of the victims!" Her breath was running rapid, "Make sure that no other such case goes without justice or gets delayed. Maintain a list of offenders publicly available and ensure they are also provided an opportunity to reform either during or after their punishment sentence is served," she paused, "And, until all the demands are met and taken care of," she breathed into the phone, "The fight continues, Inspector Rithika and not just in India but I am going to take it global! Starting from the sin city of Amsterdam…" She hung up.

www.ingramcontent.com/pod-product-compliance
Lightning Source LLC
Chambersburg PA
CBHW060546160726
47991CB00001B/454